# The Secret Files of
# FAIRDAY MORROW

# The Secret Files
## of
# FAIRDAY MORROW

### JESSICA HAIGHT & STEPHANIE ROBINSON

*Illustrations by* **ROMAN MURADOV**

**A YEARLING BOOK**

Text copyright © 2015 by Jessica Haight and Stephanie Robinson
Cover art and interior illustrations copyright © 2015 by Roman Muradov

All rights reserved. Published in the United States by Yearling, an imprint of Random House Children's Books, a division of Penguin Random House LLC, New York. Originally published in hardcover in the United States by Delacorte Press, an imprint of Random House Children's Books, a division of Penguin Random House LLC, New York, in 2015.

Yearling and the jumping horse design are registered trademarks of Penguin Random House LLC.

randomhousekids.com

Educators and librarians, for a variety of teaching tools, visit us at RHTeachersLibrarians.com

The Library of Congress has cataloged the hardcover edition of this work as follows:
Haight, Jessica.
The secret files of Fairday Morrow / Jessica Haight and Stephanie Robinson. – First edition.
pages cm.
Summary: When eleven-year-old Fairday Morrow and her family move from Manhattan to the infamous Begonia House in the quiet country town of Ashpot, Connecticut, weird clues could lead to big trouble for Fairday and the rest of the Detective Mystery Squad.
ISBN 978-0-385-74471-3 (hc) — ISBN 978-0-375-99182-0 (glb) —
ISBN 978-0-385-39102-3 (ebook)
[1. Haunted houses—Fiction. 2. Moving, Household—Fiction. 3. Family life—Connecticut—Fiction. 4. Connecticut—Fiction. 5. Mystery and detective stories.]
I. Robinson, Stephanie. II. Title.
PZ7.1.H25 Sec 2015
[Fic]—dc23
2014027342

ISBN 978-0-385-39103-0 (trade paperback)

Printed in the United States of America
10 9 8 7 6 5 4 3 2 1
First Yearling Edition 2017

This book is dedicated to Nana and Pop.

—J.H.


To my family, friends, and students,
and to all the amazing authors out there who have
helped spark my imagination!

—S.R.

Hold on to your breath
Hold on to your heart
Hold on to your hope

—*The Wizard of Oz*

# ➤➤ ASHPOT WEEKLY ◄◄

VOLUME 5, ISSUE 333    MONDAY, OCTOBER 16, 1978

## BIZARRE TRAGEDY UNFOLDS
## AT THE BEGONIA HOUSE

by Larry Lovell

Thurston Begonia, a well-known adventurer and collector of rare antiques, was found dead yesterday afternoon after falling more than thirty feet from the third-floor balcony of his home. Sources say the details surrounding his death are puzzling. Initially, it was believed that he had taken his own life. However, after further investigation, officials have concluded that homicide cannot be ruled out. Police arrived at the scene at approximately 5:00 p.m. after receiving an anonymous tip that Thurston Begonia's life was in danger. Sergeant John Wilkenson, who found Mr. Begonia's body, said, "It was a terrible sight, like something out of a nightmare." Local residents describe Mr. Begonia as a reclusive, mysterious loner. Bigford Mason, local grocer and deli owner, told police, "Ever since Thurston's daughter, Ruby, disappeared on the day of her wedding, he's been locked up tight in that old house. No one's seen him since." Ashpot residents remain baffled by the Begonia family's ongoing misfortunes. The police continue to search for clues that may shed light on this shocking case.

# ～ONE～

## THE BEGONIA HOUSE

Fairday Morrow couldn't help empathizing with Dorothy: she was definitely not in Kansas anymore. She stared out the car window at the passing trees and fields, not quite seeing all the endless possibilities her parents talked so cheerfully about. It wasn't fair, moving to stupid Ashpot. Fairday wished she weren't leaving her life in Manhattan behind, and even though she doubted she'd find any real friends, she hoped to connect with someone in the small Connecticut town.

The Morrow family cruiser bumped and jerked down the road as Fairday's two-year-old sister, Margo, giggled noisily, bouncing along in her seat. Auntie Em, the family pug, was resting next to Fairday, letting out a light snore every now and then. Giving her dog a scratch between the ears, Fairday turned her attention back to the book resting in her lap. It was one of her most prized possessions, and just the sight of it improved her mood. She smiled as she remembered her grandma reading her *The Wizard of Oz* for the first time. Fairday was only four years old. She'd fallen in love with the characters because of the enchanting voices her grandma had used for each one. Not long after, the Morrows had adopted a puppy, and Fairday had named her Auntie Em because the little dog was always frowning like Dorothy's aunt. It was funny that even when they'd first brought her home, Auntie Em hadn't resembled Toto; she'd never had that kind of energy.

Fairday began to lose herself in the sway and motion of the ride and relaxed into the story. Suddenly, Margo belched up milk all over the backseat. "Great," Fairday muttered, grasping the book protectively to her chest, "just great."

"Oh, Margo, you're such a messy baby!" Mrs. Morrow chirped as she reached back and wiped milk off Margo's face, which now sported a wide grin. She handed the towel to Fairday. "Here you go, sweetie, wipe it off with this."

Fairday took the wet towel and dropped it on the car floor in disgust. "*Why* are we moving, again?" she asked.

"We've already gone over this, Fairday," Mr. Morrow chimed in. "Your mother and I have a wonderful vision of our family's future, and we're going to make it a reality.

With her interior design skills and my wizardry in the kitchen, the Begonia House Bed-and-Breakfast is sure to be a smash hit. Trust me, you're gonna love it!"

"Not good enough, Dad," she replied, having yet to get an answer that satisfactorily justified this kind of treachery.

"Well, my dear, it will have to do!" And with that, Mr. Morrow began to sing loudly to the song on the radio. Mrs. Morrow joined in and they were gone, off to la-la land. Fairday sat back in her seat and closed her eyes, doubting that she was "gonna love" the Begonia House, as her father had so optimistically predicted. She doubted it a lot.

The car made a sharp right turn as it began to ascend the narrow, winding road that led to the Begonia House. Fairday glanced out the window, and other than the rough road that tossed them about, she could see nothing but a tangled mesh of woods that seemed to spread over the entire hill. Margo had fallen asleep, and her parents had stopped talking, so it was quiet in the car as they trundled up and up. Finally, as the road began to level out, they reached the front gate. It was enormous and made of iron. Twisted vines were wrapped around its pointed black bars, making it look like the entrance to some kind of morbid secret garden. Across the top of the gate, in large letters, were these words:

"Weird," Fairday said. "It should say, 'Fear not living a thousand miles from civilization.'"

"Oh, now, Fairday, no eleven-year-old as clever as you ever died of ennui. That's another word for *boredom*," Mr. Morrow said. He had been an English teacher for years and was constantly throwing out "new and exciting" words to improve Fairday's vocabulary. "I'm sure you'll find lots to do here. Incidentally, this house has a pretty interesting history, very mysterious. Right up your alley, with your little club and all—the Detective Mystery Squad, right?"

"That's right!" Mrs. Morrow piped up, turning to face Fairday. "You can invite Lizzy for a sleepover, and you guys can investigate. I'm sure the library has all sorts of information on the history of the house. It's very famous in these parts, and I've even heard rumors that it's haunted. Wouldn't *that* be interesting?" Her mother winked. "After you girls have conducted a thorough investigation, you can fill me in on all the juicy details. If you find something fascinating, we can display it when we open up the Begonia House Bed-and-Breakfast."

"Humph." Fairday sulked at the mention of her best friend. Even though the thought of moving into a house that could be haunted was intriguing, the idea of running into a ghost seemed much scarier without Lizzy around.

She had met Lizzy Mackerville in the first grade, when Lizzy had moved into Fairday's neighborhood. At school they had caught sight of each other's books and realized they had the same taste in stories. During recess, the other kids had made fun of Lizzy because she said *You betcha* and her accent was different. Fairday had admired how the new girl shrugged off the comments, explaining that everyone in Minnesota talked like her, and her classmates would all sound funny if they moved there. Lizzy's natural confidence made it easy to be friends with her, and from that day on she and Fairday were inseparable.

Lizzy was short and round, making her seem jolly. Bouncy blond curls framed her heart-shaped face, and she had a bubbly disposition. Fairday was the exact opposite of Lizzy. She was tall and lean, with long black hair that had a mind of its own, so it was always pulled back in a loose ponytail. Her pale face had never had the usual amount of cute baby fat most people cooed over and pinched.

One feature Fairday liked about herself was her eyes. They were an unusual charcoal gray and the reason she had such an uncommon name. Her mother said Fairday's eyes reminded her of the swirling tides of blue-gray waters that swelled up onto the sandy shores of Nantucket, where she'd grown up. When the weather was less than pleasant on the island, the fishermen would inform the tourists who came to charter their boats, "Jus' waitin' on the fair day t'morrow." And so Fairday was named Fairday Theresa Morrow, or Fairday T. Morrow. Whenever she met new kids, she had to field some annoying criticism in school about it, which went something like, "Fairday? What kind of a name is that?" or "Fairday? More like Bad Hair Day." But she didn't care. She liked the story, and she liked her name.

Mr. Morrow found the gate key, which was as black and bizarre-looking as the gate itself, and held it up for everyone to see. It had sharp, skeletal teeth, and the handle was shaped like some sort of grim flower. He made a drumroll on the steering wheel before he exclaimed, "Here we go! I am now opening the gateway to our future!"

He climbed out of the car and walked over to the gate. The key slid easily into the lock, which resembled a wide, gaping mouth, and it clicked as he gave it a turn. He pushed the heavy double gates, and they slowly swung open.

The family was quiet as the car passed through the iron barricade. Auntie Em peered out the window, her nose pressed against the glass. Even Margo was wide-eyed and straining against her car seat straps to check out the scenery. The woods began to thin as they continued toward the house. The drive was now less bumpy, and thankfully they were no longer going up. Mr. Morrow turned the car around a corner, and the outline of an enormous house came into view.

"Here we are!" he said, pulling to the center of the circular drive before putting the car in park. He turned in his seat to face Fairday. "Is it as big as you thought it would be?"

"Uh, yeah," Fairday mumbled as she looked up at the crooked house. "And just as creepy," she added.

"Well, let's get a move on," Mr. Morrow said as he pushed open the car door.

Mrs. Morrow pulled Margo out of the car seat and lifted her over her shoulder. Margo squealed, pointing at the house. "Uggy, Mommy!"

"See, even Margo thinks it stinks," Fairday said.

Mrs. Morrow laughed. "Yes, it's not as beautiful as it once was, I'm sure—"

"But," Mr. Morrow interrupted, "it will be!" He gave Mrs. Morrow a kiss, made a silly face at Margo, and patted Fairday on the head. "Let's leave our trunks here for now and come back for them after we've had a chance to investigate our new abode. *Abode* is another word for *dwelling,* Fairday." He located the right key and, once again, held it up.

Fairday rolled her eyes. Her father loved to overemphasize everything. *Enough with the key drama,* she thought. "We get it, Dad," she said. "New house, key to the future. Can we just go inside now?"

Mr. Morrow unlocked the door without saying anything else. Fairday felt terrible. "I'm sorry. I'm just missing our old home, and it was a long drive," she said, and hugged her father.

"I know, sweetie. It's a big move. It will take some time to adjust, but I promise you, this is going to be a real adventure for all of us," he said, and squeezed Fairday tight.

# TWO

## A DISTURBING NOTE

The Morrows gave each other a nervous look and then walked through the double-door entrance of the Begonia House. Auntie Em waddled into the room, sniffed a few times, and as usual, plopped down in a corner and began to snore. *Whoa,* thought Fairday. *This is definitely going to be different from our town house in Manhattan.* She scanned her surroundings; it all seemed impossibly huge and frighteningly old. They were standing in a gigantic foyer with a high ceiling and a wide staircase that spiraled down from the upper level. The cracked black-and-white-checkered floor was coated with a thick layer of filth. Hanging from the ceiling was a crystal chandelier that was so covered in dust it looked like a tinkling blob floating ominously above them.

Time seemed to have stopped. Fairday couldn't believe the size of the place or how dirty it was. The wallpaper was crumbling, and there were cobwebs hanging from every corner. Even the ancient light fixtures were creepy; they reminded her of those fake candles people put out at Halloween. The air had a stale, funny smell that she couldn't quite identify, something like burnt popcorn. A cold breeze blew through the doorway and sent a chill down her spine, the hair standing up on the back of her neck. Fairday shivered.

Margo began to wail, snapping everyone out of their trance, and time sped back up to normal. "Okay! Lots to do, lots to do," said Mr. Morrow, clapping his hands.

"Fairday, why don't you go and pick out your bedroom while I change Margo. There are quite a few to choose from," said Mrs. Morrow. She smiled at Fairday and then turned to head back out to the car. "Someone needs a fresh diapy, don't they? My smelly little oogles," she said, rubbing Margo's nose with her own, then disappearing through the door.

As Fairday climbed to the second floor, it sounded like every step was shouting a warning that it was about to give way. The upstairs hallway was lit by flickering sconces, which cast an eerie glow over paintings of people dressed in fancy, old-time clothes. As she walked past them, their eyes seemed to watch her surreptitiously. It made Fairday feel a little uneasy to be under such bizarre scrutiny.

As it turned out, Mrs. Morrow was right. The family's wing of the bed-and-breakfast had quite a few rooms to choose from. Fairday counted a total of eight doors. There were four on the right and three on the left, and there was one at the end of the hall that had a padlock hanging from it. Puzzled, she walked over and pulled down on the lock to see if it would open, but no such luck.

Abandoning that door, she began opening some of the others. One led to a bathroom that was decorated with striped silver-and-gold wallpaper, another opened to a closet that housed the world's oldest-looking mop and bucket, and yet another led to what she guessed must have been an office, judging by the antique desk and chairs covered in sheets. The remaining four rooms were bedrooms. All of them were big and had windows draped in long velvet curtains.

The drapes in the room Fairday chose were maroon with silver stripes. A circular carpet with a picture of a lion and a unicorn covered the floor. She thought it was the least gaudy of all the bedrooms and kind of liked the carpet. Her window overlooked the backyard, which was covered with yellow grass and contained one old weeping willow. "Well, this is it, I guess," she said, looking down at the depressing yard.

Fairday left the room and was heading back down the hall when she heard the strangest sound. It was faint, and it was coming from behind the padlocked door. She walked over and put her ear up against it. Something that sounded like music was coming from behind the door, but really odd music. It was high-pitched and whiny. Was she imagining it? She listened for a minute, trying to think of what could possibly make sounds like that, and then she knew. A few years back, her father had taken her to a Scottish festival in the city. She could picture the men onstage dressed in kilts and playing the bagpipes. The sound they made was unforgettable. It was beautiful but melancholy at the same time. Fairday remembered her father laughing about how he hoped it wasn't going to be a windy day. He had explained that it was an old joke that Scottish men didn't wear anything under their kilts, and if a strong wind were to blow, the audience would all get to see more than they had paid for. Fairday couldn't believe there were people who didn't wear any underwear. Luckily, it had been a calm day, and the men onstage all kept their skirts on.

Suddenly, there was a long, earsplitting note from behind the locked door. Fairday jumped back. She definitely was *not* imagining this. Someone was behind the door playing the bagpipes!

She turned and ran, her feet flying down the stairs. In her haste, Fairday accidentally tripped over Auntie Em and bumped into her father. Jolting awake, the dog let out a confused bark, looked around in surprise, and settled back into her snoring.

"Whoa there, missy! Where's the fire?" Mr. Morrow said, catching Fairday by her shoulders.

"Dad! Dad!" she said, breathing hard. "There's someone else in the house!"

"What! Where?" Mr. Morrow asked.

"Upstairs! There's a door, and I heard music or something coming from behind it!" Fairday exclaimed.

"Okay, okay! Nobody panic. Let's go up and see," Mr. Morrow said, running his fingers through his unruly black hair.

"What's going on?" Mrs. Morrow asked. She had just come through the front door with Margo.

"Fairday heard something upstairs, honey. I'm going up to check it out. You two stay down here." He motioned for Mrs. Morrow and Margo to stay put. "Come on, Fairday, let's go see what it was."

"Wait, Dad." She stopped him. "The door has a padlock on it."

"Hmm, locked, eh?" Mr. Morrow reached into his pocket and pulled out the key ring. He looked at each key and then said, "Aha! This one looks like it *could* fit a padlock." He grabbed her hand, and Fairday gave his a squeeze as they walked up the stairs.

# ~ THREE ~

## BEHIND THE LOCKED DOOR

Mr. Morrow and Fairday stood with their ears pressed against the door. "I don't hear anything anymore," she said after a few moments. "I swear I heard bagpipe music coming from behind there, Dad."

"I believe you, but I don't hear anything either. Let's open it up and find out," he said. The key he had fit the padlock, and after opening the door, they peered into the room. It was empty. There was no weird hobo piping away on the bagpipes and no ghostly specter floating about the room. It was just a circular area with a cracked stained-glass window and a spiral staircase.

Fairday felt a little let down. She shrugged. "Uh, I guess it was just the wind coming through the crack in the window or some—"

"Oh! That's right, I forgot!" Mr. Morrow interrupted her. "These are the stairs to the third floor."

"What's up there?" Fairday asked.

Mr. Morrow smiled down at her. "Looks like there's more to this house than meets the eye, eh?" He chuckled and started to climb the staircase. "Fear not the unexpected!" he announced, holding a finger in the air. "Well, come on, then, and be careful. Some of these steps look rickety."

The stairs led to an archway that opened to a short hall with a door on either side. Directly in front of them stood something covered with a yellow sheet. Fairday watched as her father walked over and pulled it off, revealing a mirror. When the dust settled, she jumped with fright. She was looking right at herself, but for a second, Fairday thought she saw two red, glimmering shoes stepping backward through a door behind them. She spun around but found only the open archway and the spiral staircase. Was she seeing things? How had that door appeared? And *who* was behind it wearing sparkling red shoes?

Fairday's fleeting thoughts were interrupted when her father cried, "Ah!" and pointed at the mirror. "Well, at least it isn't a bagpipe-playing burglar." He nodded at Fairday's shocked reflection looking back at them.

"What a weird mirror," Mr. Morrow said. "It's kind of

pretty. I could clean it up for you if you want it in your bedroom."

"No thanks," Fairday said. "I'm not into possessed mirrors."

"Maybe it's possessed by someone cool." Mr. Morrow laughed and patted her head as he turned to open the door on the right side of the hallway.

*Ugh! Dad, the eternal comedian,* Fairday thought as she rolled her eyes and followed him into the room.

"Would you look at all this stuff!" said Mr. Morrow. The room was as large as the bedrooms on the second floor but was packed with boxes, covered furniture, and odds and ends.

"This is really bizarre," Fairday said, picking up a doll with a cracked head and one glassy, staring eye. "Whose stuff is this, anyway?"

"I don't know for sure. The previous owners', I presume. You can come up here later to check it all out. I need to get back to unpacking or your mother will kill me," he said, and Fairday followed him out of the room.

"Well now, young lady, let's see what fabulous prizes we have for you behind door number two. Whoa!" Mr. Morrow exclaimed as a crisp breeze blew in, freshening up the stale air. The door opened onto a small balcony. He gingerly placed one foot on the wooden boards, which creaked and bowed under his weight. Stepping quickly back inside, he tried each key in the lock, but none was a match. He placed a hand on Fairday's shoulder. "I don't want you out there. It doesn't look safe. Since I'm not sure which key locks this door, I'll have to seal it the minute I get a chance. Until then, just picture an intimidating sign on it that says 'Stay Out.'" Then he added, "You know what *intimidating* means, right? *Intimidating* is someone or something filling you with fear."

"Sure, Dad, I get it," Fairday said. She had no plans to plummet down the back side of the house and break her neck. Incidentally, Fairday did know what the word *intimidating* meant. What she couldn't possibly know then was just how familiar with its definition she was soon to become.

# FOUR

## LOST AND FOUND

Fairday wasn't sleeping well her first night at the Begonia House. Tossing and turning, she listened to the sounds of her new surroundings. The old house clanged and groaned as the wind wrestled the willow tree outside her window. Lightning cracked as the branches banged into one another, casting monstrous shadows along the walls. A crash of thunder jolted her upright and a flash of light lit up the room. In that instant, Fairday caught sight of a figure standing at the end of her bed. Everything went dark as she pulled the blankets up to her chin in terror.

Reaching for the flashlight that was strategically positioned beneath her pillow, she shined it all around her room. No one was there. Had she been imagining things?

Fairday could've sworn she saw someone but supposed it might've been a trick of the mind. Maybe she was dreaming about Muriel from *Fablehaven*, which she'd been reading before bed. A chill ran down her spine when she noticed her door was open. She was sure her dad had closed it after saying good night. Fairday used all her courage to sneak over and shut the door. Leaping back into bed, she invoked the power of the flashlight, but the room proved to be devoid of intruders, except, of course, for herself.

Exhausted from trying to sleep, Fairday was up early the next morning. She knew her thoughts had probably just been running wild after the events of the day before. She went downstairs and found her father up and about. He was sorting through some boxes on the kitchen counter, grumbling under his breath. "Where is that toaster? Hmmm, maybe in ... AH!" Mr. Morrow shouted, jumping back when he noticed Fairday standing in the doorway. "You scared your old man half to death!" he laughed.

"Sorry, Dad." Fairday pulled the toaster out of a box and handed it to her father. "Looking for this?"

"Aha!" Mr. Morrow said. "You're up early on this dreary Sunday."

"Yeah, I didn't sleep very well last night." Fairday yawned.

"Bizarre new house and all," she said, handing her father a couple of slices of bread.

Mr. Morrow popped them into the toaster and pushed the knob down. "There! One feat accomplished!" he said, and pretended to wipe sweat off his brow.

"So, what's happening today?" she asked, smiling at her father's antics as she pulled herself onto the countertop and crossed her ankles. Auntie Em was wagging her stubby tail for a treat. Fairday noticed that the cookie jar had been unpacked and tossed her a biscuit.

"I would say you should go and explore the grounds, but unfortunately it looks like it's going to pour any minute. Why don't you check out that room on the third floor? I bet there's some neat stuff up there." Catching the toast that popped out of the toaster, he added sternly, "Remember, Fairday, do not go out onto that balcony no matter what. I mean it."

"Don't worry, Dad, I won't." Fairday nodded. She grinned at her father, adding, "I guess sifting through all that junk *could* turn out to be *mildly* interesting."

Mr. Morrow winked at her, and Fairday launched herself off the counter. In the exuberant manner of her father, she exclaimed, "Here I go! Off to reveal the mysteries of the Begonia House! I shall uncover all of the dark skeletons hidden in its many closets!" She grabbed a piece of toast and stuffed it into her mouth before dashing out of the kitchen.

Auntie Em barked her approval as Mr. Morrow laughed

theatrically. "There goes Fairday T. Morrow! The world's greatest detective!"

Fairday stopped off in her bedroom and walked over to the trunk, which was thrown in the middle of the room and still packed. She clicked it open, revealing a black backpack with the initials *DMS* sewn in gold thread across the flap. Hanging off the strap was a badge that announced in bold black letters:

### FTM, SENIOR INVESTIGATOR
### DETECTIVE MYSTERY SQUAD

Fairday set the backpack on the floor and unzipped all the pockets to check that the tools were in order. She reviewed the pack's contents, running her fingers lightly over each item while taking inventory. Fairday's DMS pack contained one slightly scratched magnifying glass, three well-used artist brushes, two ink pads, a half-filled jar of fingerprinting powder, a small black leather flip-up notebook with a pen, and one small flashlight. Lizzy's pack contained some of the tools that the DMS used on a regular basis, such as a strap-on headlamp, brand-new binoculars, an older but fairly good digital camera, and Lizzy's older brother Mark's multitool key chain, which Fairday recalled had come in handy more than once. She wished she had someone to dote on her and give her little treasures. Fairday guessed that was the difference between being the baby of the family and being the oldest.

Certain she had everything she needed, Fairday zipped up her pack, slung it over her shoulders, and exited the bedroom. She wound her way up the spiral staircase that led to the third floor, and when she reached the top step she jumped when she found Mirror Fairday staring back. Luckily there was no sign of the mysterious door. The memory of a quick flash of red shoes materialized in her mind's eye. Not wanting her imagination to get the better of her, she brushed away the strange vision.

Opening the door on the right, she slowly began to climb into the cluttered room and noticed a large object in the corner. It was covered with a sheet, and she stumbled her way over to it. "Voilà!" Fairday exclaimed, pulling the sheet off with a flourish, feeling dramatic like her dad. At that moment, the walls seemed to ripple around her, and she felt off balance. Dropping her DMS pack to the floor, she fell onto the flattened cushion of the chintz armchair she had just uncovered. Was she imagining things? Had the walls really just moved?

Sitting there quietly, Fairday steadied herself. Now everything seemed normal as she observed the messy room, which had a gloomier feeling about it this morning. It was also quite dusty and stale, smelling of mold, but Fairday was intrigued by a place that was filled with someone else's life, someone else's secrets. One corner contained a toppling stack of newspapers, and ghostly sheeted pieces of furniture were scattered about. She struggled a bit to pull herself off the cushion and sat cross-legged on the floor, setting up the DMS pack next to her. Fairday took out the notebook and pen. She flipped through a couple of pages until she came to a blank one. At the top of the page, in bold letters, she wrote:

Begonia House Inventory: The Third-Floor Room

Fairday began pulling out the contents of the nearest box. The first item she found was a tarnished silver hairbrush. She held it up and examined it. The brush had flowers and twisted vines etched into the silver. On the back, just near the base of the handle, were the initials *RB*. They were very small but elegantly engraved in looped letters. She set down the hairbrush and jotted a description of it into her notebook:

Silver hairbrush with the initials
RB engraved on the back

She thought about the initials *RB* and deduced that the *B* was most likely for *Begonia*. But what did the *R* stand for? Fairday figured it had to be a girl, as there weren't many boys who would have a hairbrush with flowers on it.

She continued to dig through the box, looking for something else that had an *RB* engraving. The next object of interest was a photo in a black oval frame. It was in color, though the glass was grimy and smudged. She wiped it off with her shirtsleeve and saw a portrait of a young woman with fiery red hair. She had an elegant face and green eyes that seemed to pop off the aged paper. The lady was sitting in a chair, which was mostly covered up by her blue dress, with her hands folded in her lap. Her lips curled up slightly at the corners, as though she knew something cryptic or classified. And in a creepy but captivating way, the piercing eyes gave Fairday the impression they were watching her.

"Hmm, I wonder who she was," Fairday said, breaking the spell that seemed to have fallen over her. She turned over the frame, slid the photo out, and grabbed the magnifying glass to get a better look. The lady's left index finger was slightly raised instead of folded in her lap and seemed to be pointing to something off in the distance. Fairday flipped the photo over and found writing scribbled at the bottom of the picture, but even with the magnifying glass she couldn't make out what it said. She would have to talk to Lizzy about this. Her best friend was amazing on the computer and could possibly create an enhanced photo of the writing so they could read it. Fairday slid it back into the frame, then set it down to log the photo into her notebook.

Small black oval frame with picture of red-haired lady. What is she pointing at? Talk to L about writing on back.

*The hairbrush could have belonged to her,* Fairday thought as she continued sifting through the box. Maybe there was something that could provide more information about the mysterious lady in the picture. Unfortunately, she found only odds and ends.

Fairday decided the time had come to unveil everything in the room. She pulled the sheets off in a swishing motion, creating puffs of dust that whirled about the room like mini-tornados. Suddenly, Fairday froze. She couldn't believe it! In the corner, peeking out from underneath a table, sat an ancient-looking bagpipe. It was covered in cobwebs and had a cracked mouthpiece. How could this be possible? She was sure she'd heard bagpipes playing just yesterday, but this instrument looked as if it hadn't been touched for years. Could the rumors be true? Was the house really haunted?

Taking a step closer, Fairday noticed an old-fashioned hourglass resting among knickknacks scattered on the table. Sparkling red sand was in both the top and bottom of the glass container. Picking it up by the tarnished silver sides, she flipped it over and gave it a shake. The sand did not drop; each grain seemed to be frozen. *Strange,* she thought. Fairday looked closer but couldn't see anything preventing it from working. Why wasn't the sand moving? Wanting to examine the hourglass further, she brought it over to her journal, made a note, then placed it carefully in her DMS pack.

The bagpipe???? Covered in cobwebs and spiders/reed gross and moldy/Could it have been played?

Silver hourglass—red sand is stuck.

A glint of gold caught Fairday's eye. A brass key was hanging over the top edge of the wardrobe. She walked over and pulled it down to find it had the same shape as the one that opened the formidable front gate of the Begonia House.

"Fairday! Time for lunch," Mrs. Morrow called from below.

"Okay, Mom," Fairday answered, thinking how fast the time had flown by. She quickly shoved the hairbrush and frame into her DMS pack, along with the brass key. Whipping the pack over her shoulder, she exited the third-floor room, banging the door closed behind her.

# ~ FIVE ~

## FOOD FOR THOUGHT

Renovations of the Begonia House began at eight o'clock sharp on Monday morning. Fairday was awake, listening to the banging of tools and sloshing of paint buckets as workers got ready to battle the crumbling walls. She could hear rushed footsteps in the hallway and knew there were going to be herds of people clattering about in the house that morning. She felt almost happy to be going to school. *Almost.*

"Fairday! Time to get up and get ready!" Mr. Morrow yelled from downstairs.

"All right, Dad!" she responded, but continued to lie in bed and stare at the cracked ceiling. There was so much noise in the house, Fairday couldn't hear herself think, and unfortunately, she had tons of things to think about. School had started a month ago. This was another one of her huge objections to the sudden move. She didn't know anyone in the school, and she could already picture herself fumbling around, totally lost and looking like a jerk, whereas all the other kids had had some time to get to know the routine.

Worst-case scenarios raced through her head. What if, while the teacher was introducing her to the class, she sneezed and blew boogers all over their horrified faces? Or she went to the bathroom and unknowingly picked up a long strip of toilet paper that stuck to her shoe? Or the ultimate nightmare: what if she farted loudly on the first day and was dubbed "Fairday-Farts-a-Lot" or something even worse? She shivered at the thought. Something like that could really determine what type of year you were going to have in school. Pulling herself out of bed, she tried to reel in the anxious thoughts that continued to whiz around in her brain and started getting ready.

Fairday sighed as she pulled clothes out of her trunk. Finally deciding on a blue long-sleeved shirt, her favorite pair of jeans, and her purple Converse, she felt confident she wouldn't stand out from the rest of the kids.

The other issue was the picture of the red-haired lady, which seemed to be haunting her imagination. She had taken it out of the DMS pack and placed it on her night-stand next to the brass key and hourglass. During the night, she had turned over in bed every few hours, whipped out the flashlight, and shined the light over the strange objects. Fairday watched the red sand closely; it never moved. She couldn't stop thinking about the woman's glaring green eyes and secret smile. What was she pointing to in the photo? Did the hairbrush and the bagpipes belong to her? What did the writing on the back of the picture say? What did the key open? Why didn't the sand fall? These questions, along with the anxiety she felt about going to a new school, rattled around in her mind like runaway marbles. One thing was certain—she definitely needed to talk to Lizzy.

Thirty minutes later, she hurried down the stairs, brushing past the numerous construction workers, who all smiled hastily and nodded as she passed. Auntie Em was snoozing at the bottom of the stairs, snoring blissfully, paying no attention to the activity around her. Fairday reached down and patted her on the head, glad that she could find peace in this chaos.

Mrs. Morrow peeked out of a room. "Morning, hon. Quick, quick, okay?" With a sweeping glance, she smiled approvingly, adding, "Oh, you look nice! Don't forget, we have to be at school by nine-thirty sharp." Tapping the watch on her wrist, she disappeared back behind the door as Fairday nodded in acknowledgment.

Mr. Morrow was in the kitchen, sporting his GOT FOOD? apron and dancing in front of the stove. Waving a spatula and talking with a French accent, he asked, "What would you like for breakfaaast, mademoiselle?"

Knowing she had a big day ahead of her, Fairday wanted to be full enough so her stomach wouldn't growl, but not so full she had to worry about becoming Fairday-Farts-a-Lot. "I'll have blueberry pancakes," she replied with a grin. *Can't hurt to start off the day with my favorite breakfast.* Just then, she noticed that the laptop had been set up and was sitting on the kitchen counter. "Dad, can I send a quick email to Lizzy while you're making breakfast?"

*"Oui, oui!"* he said, turning to face her. "Your breakfaaast will be whipped up in ten minutes!" Her dad motioned to the frying pan with the spatula and winked at her before he got back to work.

Fairday logged on and went straight to her email. Once she pulled up a new message, she began typing away furiously, her fingers flying over the keys.

L—

no time to write—on my way to my first day at my new school. ugh. ask your mom if you can come over on friday. idk what is going on in this house. it seems like something out of a tim burton movie—big iron gate with FEAR NOT THE UNEXPECTED written on it and

it's such a crooked old house. the first day i heard bagpipe music coming from behind a locked door—so
bizarre! when we opened it there was no one there
but . . . yesterday i went searching the third floor and
found a silver brush with the initials RB on it and a
picture of a red-haired lady whose eyes seem to follow
you (it has writing on the back that i can't make out). i
also found a weird gold key. and get this—i found an
ancient-looking bagpipe and there's no way it's been
played—covered in dust—so can't be what i heard.
could it? plus there's a really weird hourglass—the
sand doesn't move, like it's frozen in place. barely had
time to make a dent in the room. we have to explore
and find out more. i already started logging everything
in my notebook. don't forget your DMS pack when you
come over. what do you think? gotta go          —F

She logged off and spun around just as her dad bowed
to her, holding a plate with three perfect pancakes, ooz-
ing with blueberries and dripping with maple syrup. They
smelled heavenly. Having her favorite breakfast always
made her feel cozy, like a warm blanket was being wrapped
around her. Fairday began gobbling up her food, barely
noticing the warm, sweet, tart flavors bursting in her
mouth because she was busy thinking about what Lizzy's
response would be. Her friend was clever and could always connect the dots, even in the most complex puzzles.

Who else could have figured out that the class ferret was stealing everyone's pencils last year? The corners of her mouth slowly turned up. No matter what the day had in store for her, Fairday knew she would have an email waiting for her when she got home.

# ~SIX~

## BROCKET THE ROCKET

Ashpot Elementary stood squarely against a bright cyan sky, showing its wear and tear through its faded and worn brownish red brick. As Mrs. Morrow turned the car into the driveway that led to the visitors' lot, Fairday could see a sprawling playground lined with a mix of thick evergreens and a brilliant display of fall foliage: burnt orange, fiery red, and golden yellow leaves that rustled gently in the breeze. A sturdy wooden playscape with a long silver slide, monkey bars, and a variety of moving passages were situated behind the school. Farther back, two basketball hoops stood guard on the blacktop, along with a bright white four-square box and a large field with soccer goals at each end. *This place gives a whole new meaning to the word* recess, Fairday thought as she grabbed her backpack and hopped out of the car. The playground at her old school had been a small blacktop area with a basketball hoop and a faded four-square box. Kids usually stood around in little clusters talking and laughing, but there was never much space to play.

After being buzzed in through the front door, Fairday and her mom walked into the office. *Here we go,* Fairday thought, giving her fingers a quick cross that today would be a good one.

The secretary had short black hair and was wearing a lime-green dress. "Good morning! Hello," she welcomed them cheerfully, standing up from her desk. "I'm Mrs. Pascoe, and you must be Fairday Morrow." She looked down at Fairday with a warm, rushed smile. Mrs. Pascoe turned to Mrs. Morrow. "After I buzzed you in, I contacted Fairday's teacher. She'll be right down. Mr. Bannwell, our principal, is in a meeting right now, but I can take your paperwork and look it over. Please have a seat; it'll just be a moment." Mrs. Pascoe gestured over to the worn-out tan chairs, whose cushions had seen better days.

Fairday noticed a caption on the bulletin board that read, WHAT'S BLACK AND WHITE AND READ ALL OVER? Glancing at the bottom, she saw US! IN THE NEWS! Newspaper clippings, backed with black paper, were neatly arranged across it. Always having loved riddles, Fairday was intrigued and began looking at the articles.

Her scrutiny landed on a photograph of a man with gobs of whipped cream dripping off his beard and down the front of his shirt. Fairday squinted at the writing below it. Nudging her mother, she said, "Look at that. It's the principal, Mr. Bannwell. It says the students at Ashpot Elementary read over a hundred thousand pages as part of a reading challenge, and he agreed to have pie thrown in his face by the student who read the most books. That's hilarious!" Fairday giggled. "It makes me want to read even more!"

Before they could examine anything else on the board, the secretary called them back over. "Well, it appears everything's in order. Oh! Look! Here's Miss Mason now," said Mrs. Pascoe as a pretty brown-haired woman pushed open the office doors.

"You must be Fairday," she said, shaking Fairday's hand, then Mrs. Morrow's. "I'm Miss Mason, and I'm going to be your fifth-grade teacher. The other students are in art now but will be arriving back to the classroom momentarily. How would you like to enter the room? Do you want me to introduce you? Would you like to say a few words to the class? I want you to feel comfortable, so whatever you think is best." Her new teacher was beaming as she fired off question after question.

Fairday bit her lip, then answered, "Um, you can introduce me when we walk in, but I really don't want to say anything about myself, if that's okay."

"No problem!" Miss Mason replied. She turned toward Mrs. Morrow. "It was a pleasure to meet you. And don't worry! Fairday's in good hands."

"Nice to meet you too," Mrs. Morrow said, and turned to face Fairday. She leaned down and whispered, "Have a great first day, honey. I'm sure you'll make some really special friends, and I just know you're going to love it here. Your future awaits!"

"Bye, Mom," Fairday said quickly before giving her a little wave. She wanted to get out of the office to avoid the scene getting any more emotional. Fairday knew her mom could get very sentimental, especially when it came to this so-called new beginning they were forging ahead with.

Large windows lined one side of the hallway, allowing natural light to showcase the student artwork that hung on the opposite wall. Although the school was fairly old, it had freshly painted walls and clean surfaces, making it bright and welcoming. After a short walk, Miss Mason slowed down and gave Fairday a small smile before turning left into room 208. Directly behind her, Fairday could see posters neatly displayed below the windows and surrounding the SMART Board, with groups of desks placed throughout. A short blond woman stood monitoring the students as they munched on snacks, chatted, and took out their books. Miss Mason cleared her throat and all eyes focused immediately on her.

"Class, this is Fairday Morrow. She just moved here from Manhattan. Let's all try to help her learn about our school and procedures," Miss Mason explained in a sunny but no-nonsense tone.

Fairday looked at the class with a faint smile and mumbled, "Hi," which was followed by a variety of greetings from the students, along with a couple of chuckles and whispers. Miss Mason escorted her over to a group of four desks in the back.

As she slid into her seat, her heart was racing. She tried to appear calm and hoped she was pulling it off. The girl and two boys in her group smiled tentatively at her and then looked down. Before Fairday could even consider the stack of books on her desk, Miss Mason began the science lesson. She glanced down, wondering which one of them to open. Fairday hurried to find her place, overhearing the kids in her group whispering about an incident that had happened in art class. Apparently, someone named Olivia spilled paint on another girl named Macy, and everyone thought it had been done on purpose. Fairday couldn't add anything to the conversation, so she didn't look up. Secretly, though, she wished they would change the topic and give her an easy opening to join in. Fairday snapped her head up when she heard Miss Mason say sternly, "Marcus, I'm talking now. Please go give yourself a check."

Murmurs of "Brocket the Rocket" could be heard coming from around her table. *What kind of nickname is that?* She turned to look at the boy next to her. With his dark skin and short haircut, she couldn't see why his nickname had anything to do with rockets, and hadn't Miss Mason called him Marcus? From the panicked expression on the boy's face and the way the teacher had glared at him, Fairday concluded he had to be one and the same.

Instinctively, her hand shot into the air. Before she knew what she was saying, Fairday blurted out, "I'm sorry. He was telling me what page to turn to in our science book. I wasn't sure." She shrugged and smiled. Marcus's eyes grew wide for a split second before he put on a straight face and stared back at the teacher.

Miss Mason looked surprised and tilted her head to the side as if trying to decide whether to believe Fairday. After a short pause, she cleared her throat and said, "Okay, then. Sorry, Marcus. Thanks for helping. No check. If you could, please help Fairday throughout the day." She turned toward the SMART Board and began the lesson on invisible light.

Marcus grinned at Fairday and nodded slightly, gesturing *thank you.* It was hard to put into words what had made her raise her hand, since she normally didn't like to draw attention to herself. Fairday hadn't even been sure if a check was a bad thing, but she smiled back, thinking she might have just made her first friend.

She opened her science book, breathing an inward sigh

of relief that she'd already studied some of this information at her last school. When she'd left, they'd finished their unit on light and were just starting to learn about sound. *At least I won't look like an idiot,* she thought as Miss Mason questioned the kids about how invisible light might be used by doctors, scientists, and other professions.

Marcus immediately put his hand up. "Well, because invisible light can show things we can't see, it's used by cops, detectives, and FBI agents, like my dad. Once he let me try on his night-vision goggles, which use infrared light. It was so cool to see animals at night walking around in the woods near my house. Also, he told me the FBI uses black lights to reveal chemicals and liquids that might not be seen otherwise. His department uses them all the time." Marcus sounded proud of his dad, and Fairday couldn't blame him. She would be over-the-top excited if her dad were an FBI agent. Imagine all the amazing resources she would have at her fingertips to solve mysteries! Night-vision goggles, computer programs, listening devices ... *Wait a minute,* she thought as she realized that this Marcus Brocket kid *did* have access to all kinds of fancy detective equipment. Could he be the next Detective Mystery Squad candidate?

# ~ SEVEN ~

## A GOOD LEAD

Fairday was squeezed into a window seat in the middle section of the school bus, her backpack propped up between her and a girl with blond hair. The girl sharing her seat was deep in conversation with two girls sitting across the aisle from her. Fairday knew this had to be Olivia, as it appeared the art room scandal was still the hot topic. She could hear them whispering, "Macy said what?" and "I heard she was really upset."

As Fairday gazed out the window at the blurs of gold, red, orange, and yellow zooming by, she thought about how different the scenery was from the city. It was colorful and open compared to the towering buildings and busy streets of Manhattan. Luckily, school seemed pretty much the same. The kids were nice, and mostly normal. She liked her teacher, and it looked as though it was going to be okay. But she missed Lizzy, and every time she thought about the distance between them, it made her miserable. Fairday couldn't wait to get home and see what her best friend had written back to her. She hoped Lizzy would be able stay over for the weekend.

The bus slowed to a stop and one of the boys sitting in the back stood up. As he left his seat, he lightly punched another boy on the shoulder, announcing, "Later, Dif. Don't cry. We all know Brocket's gonna wreck you tomorrow at recess."

Snickers burst out from the back of the bus, followed by "Way to go, Banner!" and "Brocket's gonna win!"

Fairday watched the boy they were calling Banner climb down the steps and get off the bus. He was scruffy, with dirty-blond hair that was just a little bit too long and a friendly but mischievous-looking face. He stopped at the bottom of his driveway, turned around, and dramatically wagged his butt at the bus. The boys he had been sitting with were cracking up and pointing at him out the window, yelling, "Banner! Banner!" All were laughing except the boy Dif, who was scowling. She thought for a moment about what Banner had said: *"Brocket's gonna wreck you."* What did that mean? Marcus Brocket seemed all right in class, but was he some kind of bully who went around beating up kids? Fairday was suddenly unsure about her first impression of Brocket. What was going to happen at recess tomorrow?

The bus maneuvered around a curve in the road, and she was relieved to see the Morrow family cruiser parked at the corner of the steep drive that led up to the front gate. Fairday was thankful she didn't have to walk all the way up to the house. *That would be a form of torture,* she thought as she grabbed her backpack and climbed out of the seat, trying not to bump into anyone. She flashed a smile at Olivia, who hesitantly smiled back.

Fairday made it to the front of the bus and was just about to climb off when she heard a voice yell out, "Hey, Fairday!" She turned around to see who had shouted. It was Dif, looking at her from the back of the bus with a nasty smirk plastered across his face. A perfectly buzzed haircut and his camouflage army jacket made him look severe. Fairday stared back calmly as he added, "How's the haunted Begonia shack? Seen any dead people yet?"

Everyone was silent for just a moment, and then Fairday heard whispers of "She lives in that place?" and "Ugh, that place is freaky" throughout the bus.

She looked directly at Dif and replied in her most upbeat tone, "Oh, I know, right! That place is so peculiar! No dead people yet, thankfully. But I did find some really cool stuff in a secret room. Anyway, see you later!" Even though she worried what he said might be true, she smiled as she turned to get off the bus. For whatever reason, Dif had tried to embarrass her in front of the other kids, and she was sure it had totally backfired. Fairday hoped every person on the bus was now thinking about what she had found and how awesome it was that there was a secret room in her house.

Fairday waved to her mother as she climbed down the steps and jogged over to the car. As she pictured a scornful Dif staring out the window, her grin widened even more. Hopping into the car, she saw her mother's beaming face.

"So, how was it today? Tell me everything!" her mother gushed, looking expectantly at Fairday.

"It was a pretty great first day, Mom," Fairday replied, tilting her head to the side and shrugging one shoulder, relieved it was actually over and she had survived.

"Oh, honey, I knew it would be. Did you make any new friends?" her mother asked as the car started slowly up the winding drive.

"Well, it's hard to say right now, but most of the kids are okay. I sit near this boy, Marcus Brocket, and he seems interesting. Though I'm not entirely sure about him yet. No one here is like Lizzy," she said. "But I guess there's only one of her."

"You might be surprised and really click with someone here. You'll still see Lizzy. We promised we'd plan a get-together for you girls at least once a month. Her parents both agreed to alternate whose weekend with her would be missed. That was very nice of them, especially because her father doesn't get to see her very often."

"I guess," Fairday replied, missing her friend. Changing the subject, she said, "Miss Mason seems really kind and treats everyone fairly." She paused, thinking about the incident with Marcus and how her teacher had contemplated the situation for a moment before making a decision. Fairday decided to keep that part of the day to herself, but added, "She made science entertaining." She also left out the part about Dif on the bus, but as far as she was concerned, she had won that small battle and felt pleased at her own cleverness. No matter what kind of a jerk this kid Dif might be, she had set him in his place by not reacting in a defensive way and giving him the upper hand.

Fairday saw the words FEAR NOT THE UNEXPECTED as the car passed under them. She couldn't help but agree, remembering how fearful she had been that morning. It turned out there had been nothing to worry about.

"Your father's going to be thrilled your first day was so successful. He's cooking your favorite dinner tonight to celebrate. Get ready for some out-of-this-world chicken cordon bleu," her mother announced, doing her best to sound like Mr. Morrow. Fairday's mouth watered and her stomach rumbled. She hadn't realized just how hungry she was, and decided not to check the laptop to see if Lizzy had written back until after she'd eaten.

Walking into the house, she dropped her backpack by the front door to find that the clattering, banging, and sloshing of paint buckets from earlier in the morning still hadn't ceased. *This is not going to be a fast process,* Fairday thought, stepping over a ladder in the middle of the foyer and heading toward the kitchen.

Margo was sitting in her high chair eating Cheerios while her father sat at the table next to her with his nose in a book. Auntie Em was drooling by their feet, ready to snatch up any fallen treats. The afternoon sun streamed into the room, cloaking Margo's soft brown hair in a halo of light. *Ha!* thought Fairday, thinking how deceptively angelic her little sister could look. Margo was such a curious and sneaky child, always getting herself into all sorts of trouble. She wasn't exactly an angel, but everyone agreed she sure was cute. Fairday gave her sister a quick peck on the head and grabbed a couple of her Cheerios.

"Mine," Margo gurgled, pointing at the stolen cereal. Mr. Morrow looked up from his book and motioned for Fairday to come closer.

She hugged her father. "Thanks, Margo," she said, smiling in the hopes of appeasing her baby sister so she wouldn't explode into one of her famous tantrums.

"Are you famished, my dear?" her father asked, raising his eyebrows to see if she understood the vocabulary word.

"Yeah, I could go for a snack," she answered, grinning back at him. He made his way to the refrigerator and took out some cheese and crackers. As her dad sliced the cheese, she played with Auntie Em and filled him in on her first day. However, the whole time, she wondered if she had the willpower to wait a couple of hours to check her email. At least the mountain of homework and her dad's delectable dinner would keep her occupied for most of the evening.

Wiping her wet hands, Fairday hung the dish towel over the handle of the old-fashioned stove. Looking at the stove, she never would've guessed it still worked. It was white, with two electric burners on each side and a burnt griddle between them. It had a foggy-looking clock, whose old hands were pointing at three o'clock, which was definitely not the correct time. Fairday figured her dad would probably have a field day trying to figure out how to reset the antique timepiece. Mrs. Morrow had let everyone know that since all the important appliances were still functioning, it would be a while before they updated the kitchen. Fairday looked forward to having a dishwasher so she would no longer have to include dishwashing on her list of chores. At least tonight, all the scrubbing and drying had been worth it. Dinner had been delicious, and waiting a little longer to check her email had given Fairday more hope that Lizzy's response would be there.

Fairday logged on to the computer. The connection was a bit slow, and she tapped her foot while she waited for her email to pop up. Finally, one new message displayed on the screen and she clicked it open.

F—

so happy to get your email. hope the day was great.
missed you at school. mr. barkley gave a pop quiz in
math today and everyone was freaking out. my mom
said yes about this weekend. : ) thank goodness you
only moved about an hour away. she'll drive me up
after school on friday. thought about what you found
so far—v. mysterious. can't wait to explore your new
place. i may have a start b/c i put the name begonia
into google images and i found 1 picture. it's of a guy
and a lady standing in front of a unique-looking house.
pretty sure it's your house. the picture has the caption "thurston begonia unveils magnificent new home
after years of construction." i attached it for you. i think
there's something behind the willow tree. i'll work on
enhancing the picture. we'll have to go to the library
to find out more about who used to live there. already
have my dms pack ready to go. can't wait to see you.
gotta run—still have homework to do. ugh. ttyl

—L

Fairday drummed her fingers against her chin and bit her
lip. Her heart was beating quickly as she reread the email.
She clicked on the attachment and waited as the photo
downloaded and came into focus. *Wow,* she thought as it
popped up on the screen. She hadn't expected to see the Be-

gonia House looking so regal. In the image, the house was not crooked or crumbling. On the contrary, curtains hung neatly behind clean windows, and perfectly aligned shingles covered the rooftops. Flowering vines draped over the entryway, and the willow Fairday could see out her bedroom was in full leaf. The man in the picture had a broad smile on his face, his left arm wrapped around the shoulder of a pretty young woman. Fairday immediately knew this was not the red-haired lady in the photo and couldn't help feeling somewhat deflated. The man was facing the camera; his other arm was extended back toward the house, and the woman was smiling up at him, her hair falling gracefully around her slim shoulders.

*It is a sweet picture,* thought Fairday as she took note of the fluffy clouds floating above the pointed rooftop. Suddenly, she remembered Lizzy mentioning there was something behind the willow tree. She enlarged the image and scanned the right side of the picture. She couldn't see very clearly, but there was definitely an odd shadow there. Maybe it was an animal or a large bush? Fairday couldn't tell. It could be nothing. But as she squinted even harder and narrowed her gaze, a shiver ran down her spine. It looked like a face peering out, though it blended with the shadows around the trunk of the tree.

She stared at the picture for quite some time, but it was impossible to tell for certain what it was. *Weird,* Fairday thought, leaning back in her chair. Was someone secretly spying on the happy couple? And did this picture have anything to do with the red-haired lady or the initials *RB*?

# ~EIGHT~

## A TICKING BOMB

The next day, Fairday was sitting at her desk, lost in thought over the picture Lizzy had sent. She hadn't even touched the bag of veggie crisps her mother had packed as a snack. Her classmates, on the other hand, were tearing open their packages like wild animals while chatting and trying to trade up for a better bite to eat. Fairday snapped back to reality when she heard Miss Mason's voice calling her. Standing up, she crossed the room, hoping she wasn't in any sort of trouble. Nearing the teacher's desk, a welcoming smile greeted her, laying her fears to rest.

"Hi, Fairday. How's everything going so far? Any questions?" her teacher asked.

"Um, things are good," Fairday replied, flashing an honest smile. And they were, for the most part. Except for the incident on the bus, everything was rolling along pretty smoothly. Although she missed Lizzy and her old life, the first two days of school had been fine.

"Well, that's just wonderful!" Miss Mason replied. "I wanted to talk to you about a biography project the students have been working on for the past week. Your classmates have already selected someone from Ashpot they will be interviewing," she explained. "I thought, since you're new to town, I would help you get started. Would that be all right with you?"

Fairday thought for a moment and decided this assignment had the potential to be interesting. "Sure, I'd like that," she said.

"Excellent!" Miss Mason said. Leaning in close to Fairday, she lowered her voice. "My grandfather has been an Ashpot resident for over sixty years, and he was a reporter for the local newspaper, the *Ashpot Weekly*. He's retired now, but I spoke to him and he agreed to be asked a few questions."

"Thanks," Fairday answered, getting even more excited about her luck. This person *must* know who used to live in her house after working as a reporter in such a small town for so long. Hadn't her mom said the house had some mysterious local lore? The more Fairday thought about it, the more appealing this project seemed.

"His name is Larry Lovell," Miss Mason continued.

"I have a packet prepared for you with the information you'll need for the assignment." She opened the folder and showed it to Fairday. "I wrote his number here." She pointed to the top of the page, then closed the folder and handed it over.

Fairday thanked Miss Mason and walked back to her seat. Slipping the folder into her desk, she was stunned at her luck! Lizzy was not going to believe that the DMS already had the perfect contact for their investigation of the Begonia House. Things were definitely looking up.

Settling down for the remaining snack time, Fairday tore open her chips and popped one into her mouth. The chatter and munching in the room continued as she looked around the class. Marcus and Banner were talking with a group of kids. Fairday had come to learn a little about these two. Banner Parker was one of Marcus's good friends and was undoubtedly the class clown. Marcus, however, was still a bit of a mystery. With his calm, cool demeanor, she couldn't quite get a feel for him.

Fairday hadn't really spoken to Marcus since rescuing him from the dreaded check. He had tried to strike up a few conversations while helping her, but Fairday was reluctant. She was afraid of getting too chummy with him, feeling unsure about what kind of person he was. Part of her thought he might still be a candidate for the DMS, but she didn't want a bully in the group, regardless of his accessibility to stellar spy equipment. Was he really going to fight Dif? She looked away from him. Just a couple of hours until two o'clock and then all would be revealed.

Fairday noticed Dif and his friends on the other side of the classroom. Her initial feelings about him had been correct. Brian Diffren was not a nice boy. In fact, it seemed the only people who did like him were just as unpleasant as he was. This morning she had sat next to one of his cronies in library class: Sadie Moore, a mean girl who mocked everyone around her. Most of the kids in fifth grade chose to keep up appearances with Sadie, trying not to attract her attention. This girl could be downright cruel when she found an easy target. Fairday wasn't the least bit impressed by someone who made fun of other people because they were different. After all, how boring would life be if everybody were the same?

Sure enough, Sadie had eventually attempted an attack on the new girl, and Fairday had accepted the call to action. Fairday never let anyone get the better of her.

"Psst, Fairday," Sadie hissed as she passed a folded note to her under the table during library. Fairday opened it and read:

*We all think you're a loser—maybe you can make friends with the cockroaches in your house, since it's so gross!*

Fairday crumpled up the note, stood, and walked over to the trash before dropping it in. Moving back into her seat, she lightly touched Sadie's shoulder and leaned in close to whisper, "Thanks for the update, Sadie. I'll keep your advice in mind. By the way, you have something long and green hanging out of your nose. You should probably go and blow it."

That was all it took. Sadie's face turned beet-red. She hurried over to the sign-out sheet for the bathroom and grabbed the pass off the wall, covering her nose with her sleeve. Fairday sat in her seat, unmoved by the failed plot to hurt her, and continued working. A girl sitting across the table was watching, a look of incredulity on her face. Fairday had noticed Sadie harassing this girl and hoped she had inspired her to stand up for herself in the future. Fairday knew that most of the time, mean kids were just insecure, and if you didn't let them get to you, they usually left you alone. Bullies were only triumphant when they made other people feel smaller than they themselves felt.

Dif's other cohort was Bart Monahan, and he was almost as big a jerk as Dif. Bart had the same obnoxious air about him but lacked Dif's severity. Rather, he was clumsy, with messy black hair and thick, bushy eyebrows. He followed Dif around like a lost puppy. He could usually be heard saying things like "Real cool, dorkwad" or "What an L-O-S-E-R," spelling it out and holding his thumb and forefinger up to his forehead in an L shape. At least he could spell, thought Fairday.

Dif, Bart, and Sadie were now all huddled in a corner of the room, glaring at Marcus and his friends. Marcus was laughing, not paying them any mind.

"You're gonna kill Dif today," Banner said.

Marcus gave him two thumbs up and said, "Hey, they don't call me Brocket the Rocket for nothing!" Everyone at the table cheered and patted him on the back.

Fairday lowered her gaze from the scene. She didn't like violence, and the thought of witnessing a fight was unsettling. She was beginning to wonder if her first impression of this school had been a bit off. The one thing she couldn't figure out was the nickname. What did rockets have to do with fistfighting? Maybe he had a really powerful right hook or something?

The buzz of voices began to quiet as Miss Mason took her place at the front of the class. Glancing again at Dif, Fairday saw him sitting straight up at his desk, chin jutting forward as he stared at Marcus. Marcus held Dif's stare and nodded. Fairday let out a sigh of relief when Miss Mason asked everyone to take out their math materials. At least adding fractions would keep her mind off the upcoming event.

As the students of room 208 walked down the hall, you could feel the anticipation in the air. A suppressed energy was just below the surface, but Fairday felt like she could actually touch it. An aide held open the door of the school and the class began running out to the field. Fairday walked toward the playground amid the frenzy of activity. Dif strode past and bumped into her, causing Fairday to stumble. He glowered back with an ugly sneer. "Any ghosts yet, Freakday?"

Not missing a beat, she replied, "Whatever," and waved him off. Fairday continued walking through the throng of children. Marcus pushed past her, following right behind Dif. He slowed for a moment and turned to her. Shaking his head, he rolled his eyes in exasperation at Dif's comment. Marcus picked up his pace and hurried off toward the field. Fairday just didn't get it; Marcus seemed so nice. Didn't he understand that fighting proved nothing?

Fairday was astounded by what was happening around her. Everyone was pushing and shoving, lining up on the sidelines, all getting ready to watch Marcus kill Dif. It seemed so medieval. She vowed to herself that she wouldn't watch. Lizzy would never go for this sort of thing. Hanging back from the other kids, Fairday stood away from all the action. Even though she wanted to fit in at this new school, she couldn't bring herself to be somebody she wasn't.

The crowd was going wild. A chubby boy with red hair and a smattering of freckles across his nose was pumping his fists in the air chanting, "Rock-et! Rock-et!" Next to him stood Olivia, her blond hair shimmering in the afternoon sun. She was clapping her hands and turning her head occasionally to whisper and giggle with a group of girls standing around her.

Within moments, a voice yelled, "Ready . . . set . . . go!" The scene exploded. Kids were screaming and yelling; the sound was deafening. "Go, Brocket! You're wasting him!" echoed through the air, followed by "Brocket the Rocket!" and "He's on fire!" Fairday looked over at the two aides, expecting to see them run over to stop the boys from killing each other. Amazingly, they, too, were enthralled with what was happening. Both women were pointing to the field.

Fairday looked back at the commotion and couldn't believe her eyes. Marcus Brocket was a green blur flying down the field, arms pumping up and down, his long strides making him look like an Olympic runner. This wasn't a fight; it was a race! Behind him, Dif was panting, his face pink with exertion as he tried with all his might to catch up. Marcus was beating the pants off Dif, and Fairday couldn't have felt happier about it. All of her anxiety disappeared, and she found herself caught up in the action. She hurried over to the side of the field and joined the bustling crowd just as Marcus crossed the finish line. Her classmates were all cheering, jumping up and down excitedly, and exclaiming, "Whoo-hoo! Rocket rules!"

Marcus jogged over to his friends with an ear-to-ear grin on his face as Dif slunk off to the side. Suddenly, it clicked. The nickname Brocket the Rocket didn't have to do with being a bully at all; it had to do with speed, being fast, like a rocket blasting off. She looked up at Marcus, pleased that her first impression about him had been right, and she was intrigued at the prospect of a new friend who could peacefully put a bully in his place. "Way to go," Fairday said, catching Marcus's eye as he wiped the sweat off his face. She smiled at him and he winked back, sporting a gleaming winner's grin.

# ~NINE~

## A PECULIAR WARNING

It wasn't until after school on Thursday that Fairday had the chance to call Larry Lovell. She grabbed the phone off the kitchen counter, closed the door to block out the noisy construction, and sat down at the table. Fairday bit down on her lip as she opened the project folder. Taking a deep breath, she dialed the number Miss Mason had written down. Her heart was thudding against her chest as she anticipated an answer. Three rings later, a gruff, old man's voice said, "H'llo?"

"Hi, is Mr. Lovell there, please?" Fairday asked much too quietly, her palms growing sweaty.

"Eh? Speak up, there. Who's this?" the voice replied with a hint of irritation.

Gathering herself, she repeated, though much louder this time, "Um. Hi, hello. This is Fairday Morrow. May I please speak to Mr. Lovell?" Nothing. Pressing on courageously, she continued. "My, uh, teacher, Miss Mason, gave me this number so I can interview him for a biography project we're working on in class?" Her uncertainty made the statement come out sounding like a question.

"Eh?" A hesitation, a muttering sound, and then, at last, a spark of realization. "Oh, yes! Fairday, Fairday Morrow. Maggie did mention something. I remember thinking how unusual that name is." He cleared his throat. Fairday clung to the phone as his voice came back. "Yes, yes, this is Larry Lovell."

Breathing a sigh of relief, she relaxed her grip on the phone. "Well, thanks for agreeing to be interviewed. I'm looking forward to meeting you. Do you have any free time this weekend?" she asked, feeling more confident now.

"It's not a problem," he mumbled. "Saturday mornings I'm at the library. Can you be there at ten o'clock?"

Fairday would have to check with her parents, but she didn't think it would be a problem. "Sure. That would be great. It's not too far. My family and I just moved into the old Begonia House."

"D-did you say the B-Begonia House?"

"Yeah. I don't know if you're familiar with it?" She felt a rush of excitement as she waited for his response. From the moment Miss Mason told her about him, she'd been hoping he would know something about her house and its previous occupants.

"Oh yes. I am quite familiar with that house." His voice turned grave as he added, "Quite familiar indeed. I wasn't aware anyone had moved in there," he murmured. "Yes, yes, this is very intriguing. Well, young lady, now I find myself compelled to ask you a few questions when we meet."

Fairday gnawed at her bottom lip, contemplating what kinds of questions he would ask her. What could she possibly answer for him? Suddenly realizing he was still hanging on, she replied, "Well, I guess I'll see you Saturday, and thanks again for agreeing to work with me."

"No, dear, thank *you*. I must say you've given me a bit to think on." Larry's voice became stern as he added, "Be careful, Miss Morrow. Please be very careful." She heard a click, and he was gone.

Fairday stood holding the phone midair, her mouth open. What did he mean? Who or what did she have to be careful of?

Fairday had planned to visit the library with Lizzy to research the home's history. This was the icing on the cake, interviewing someone who actually knew about the Begonia House, besides the convenient point that she *had* to do all this for a project. Things were coming together. Saturday was going to be chock-full of surprises.

Scribbling down the meeting time, she skipped over to the laptop to email Lizzy. Keeping her partner informed about all the latest developments was top priority. Her eagerness about the upcoming weekend empowered her fingers to move in rapid keystrokes, and her thoughts flew onto the screen. She wrote about Marcus Brocket being a prospect for the DMS, including the fact that he had access to all sorts of detective equipment. Also, she touched on Marcus's "rocket"-fast speed. Then she whipped off an abbreviated version of her conversation with Larry Lovell and mentioned the meeting at the library. Lizzy would be thrilled to hear about a potential new DMS member, and Fairday was sure she'd compile a list of intelligent questions to ask their interviewee.

Just as she clicked the send button, Mr. Morrow strode into the kitchen, doing his best impersonation of a train conductor, announcing that the gravy train was just about to pull into the station. Fairday turned and smiled up at her father, knowing this was his unique way of saying dinner was about to be served.

# ~ TEN ~

## THINGS AREN'T WHAT THEY SEEM

Mr. Morrow had outdone himself once again with a masterful cuisine of cheesy baked macaroni. Fairday felt satisfied and full as she placed the last dried dish back in the cabinet. Briefly glancing over at the hazy broken clock next to it, she noticed the time was still stuck at exactly three o'clock. *Hmm. I wonder why it's stopped.* After all, the clock didn't run on batteries; the stove was electric, and it was plugged into the same outlet, working perfectly fine. Had it stopped telling time at three in the morning or three in the afternoon? Fairday concluded there was no way to tell for sure. Was there any significance to that time? She made a mental note to jot it down in her DMS notebook and to ask her dad if he had tried to fix the clock yet, just in case it turned out to be important.

Now that dinner was done and her homework was completed, Fairday decided to get to work on the case. Knowing her parents would be preoccupied with fixing the house, she was looking forward to having a little more time to herself. Heading upstairs, she stopped in her room and grabbed her DMS pack. As she walked toward the door at the end of the hall, she couldn't help but notice the painted faces hanging along the walls. Once again, she had the weird sensation of being monitored by their oily eyes.

The door creaked open, and Fairday began to climb the spiral staircase. Halfway up the winding steps, she suddenly heard the soft sound of bagpipes. Stopping dead in her tracks, she listened closely. The notes were sour and echoed around her for only an instant. The hair on the back of her neck stood up. Just then she heard her mother's voice calling out to her. Mrs. Morrow's hurried footsteps padded down the second-floor hallway. Breathlessly, she called out again, "Fairday, honey, where are you?"

Fairday twisted around on the stairs, answering, "I'm here, Mom," her voice shaking a bit. Stepping down, she walked back to the door and peeked her head out.

"There you are! I swear, this place is like a maze!" Mrs. Morrow exclaimed, pushing back her smooth brown hair and adjusting Margo on her hip.

"Did you hear that noise a second ago?" Fairday blurted out.

"What noise, honey? Are you okay?" Mrs. Morrow reached out and lifted Fairday's chin tenderly.

"I thought I heard . . . Um, I guess it was nothing." Fairday shrugged, biting her thumbnail, worried that it was all in her head.

"Are you sure? You seem shaken."

"Yeah, I'm okay."

"All right, honey. I'm so sorry. I know you're getting ready for Lizzy's visit tomorrow, but I have so much to get together with the house right now." She paused, looking apologetically down at Fairday, and added in a hushed voice, "Can you please watch Margo for a little while? Dad needs some time on the computer, and I don't want to disturb him."

*Ugh,* she thought, annoyance creeping over her. Fairday loved her sister, but there would be no real investigative work accomplished with Margo around. Sometimes being an older sister meant less time for herself. Reluctantly she replied, "Sure, Mom," forcing a smile and stepping out of the doorway.

"Thanks, honey! I really appreciate it. And I'll make sure you girls have all the space you need this weekend. I just changed Margo's diaper and gave her a snack, so she should be pretty settled. You can bring her up there with you, if you want." She motioned to the door behind Fairday as she handed Margo over. "But *please, please* make sure she stays out of trouble." Fairday completely understood her mother's concern; Margo could be a handful at times. Her mother spun around on her heels, adding, "Love you!" as she rushed down the hall.

Toting her sister in one arm and her DMS pack over the other, Fairday pushed open the door at the end of the hall with her foot. Margo's head was turning left and right, eyes wide, as they wound up and up. When they reached the open archway, Margo caught sight of her own reflection in the mirror and pointed at it, shouting, "ME!"

Fairday smiled, admiring her sister's bravery as she remembered jumping in fright when she first saw herself reflected in it. But there had been something very strange about her reflection that time. Fairday could have sworn she saw a door, slightly ajar, appear in the mirror. And two sparkling red shoes had been hastily retreating behind it. With everything else that had been happening, she had almost forgotten about that bizarre vision. She had chalked it up to her runaway imagination. But maybe there *was* something peculiar about that old mirror.

With a suspicious glance at it, she turned to the right and opened the door to the cluttered room. She gently set Margo on the floor. But before her sister could get a head start and run for the stairs or someplace else that was incredibly naughty, Fairday quickly turned and shut the door. Stepping in farther, she heard a crinkling under her foot and looked down to see what she had stepped on. She was surprised to

find dried rose petals scattered across the floor. *Odd, these weren't here before.* Reaching down, she picked one up, and it crumbled in her hand. *Where could they have come from?*

The sound of Margo knocking over the nearest empty cardboard box brought Fairday's attention back to her little sister. As Margo crawled inside, Fairday pulled up the flap and pointed. "Okay, missy, now BE-HAVE!" Fairday accentuated the *behave* to make it sound like she was definitely the one in charge.

Margo popped out, smiling. And in her most matter-of-fact baby voice, she confirmed, "Mar-go BE-HABE. Okay, Far-fay." Her tone suggested that Fairday was absolutely silly to think she would do anything other than act like an angel.

"Okay, as long as we understand each other," Fairday said, patting Margo's head just before it ducked back into the box.

With one eye on her sister, she sat on the floor and unzipped the DMS pack. Pulling out the notebook and pen, she flipped to the pages containing the list of items she had uncovered and wrote down the latest clues:

> Time on stove clock: 3:00—Does this
> mean anything? Ask Dad if he tried to
> fix it.
>
> Dried rose petals on the floor of secret
> room—weren't there before.

They might be nothing, but best to keep track of everything that could be important. The DMS prided themselves on having all the facts straight.

Margo was still shuffling around in her newfound fort as Fairday began searching the room once again. She walked over to the bagpipe stuffed in the corner. "Ew, gross," she mumbled as she picked it up and the cobwebs stretched off in long, sticky strands, the spiders scurrying away to darker places. It was pretty nasty, she thought, setting the instrument down on a table. The reed inside the mouthpiece was disgusting, tinged brown and green with mold. The red-and-black-plaid print was faded and worn, with holes gnawed through the fabric. Probably where all the spiders lived, she guessed.

Taking out her magnifying glass and flashlight, Fairday examined the instrument, though she tried not to touch it too much. After several minutes of close observation, she confirmed there was no possible way it had been played. But the more she recalled the music, the more she worried where these sounds were actually coming from. *Maybe I'm going crazy.* Opening the notebook once again, she updated her findings and conclusions, which at this point didn't add up to much:

The bagpipe??? Covered in cobwebs and spiders/reed gross and moldy. Could it have been played? Is it a recording? *heard when we moved in (Sat.) and again today (Thurs.).

Fairday reread her notes and mused over the printout of the picture Lizzy had emailed. Her mind skipped to the mysterious shadow behind the willow tree. What exactly happened in this house? And who was Thurston Begonia? She was caught up in her thoughts, questions circling around like a carousel, when suddenly, a strange laugh broke through the silence. Her heart stopped. Jumping up, she scanned the room and saw the door was open. Hadn't she shut it? She couldn't hear Margo gurgling or bumping into anything. Where was she?

Fairday frantically raced over to the box and pulled up the flap. Nothing. *Oh God!* she thought. She couldn't move fast enough, and ran out of the room. What she saw made her scream, "NO!" Unbelievably, in the mirror's reflection, Margo was crawling through a door. She spun around, but there was only the empty archway. "What?" Fairday yelled, utterly confused. Turning back to look into the mirror, she couldn't believe her eyes. Margo was almost gone, practically all the way through the opening of the nonexistent door. Without thinking, she dropped to her knees and stuck one arm into the mirror. "This is crazy!" she cried as her arm went right through the glass, which seemed to liquefy. Stretching as far as she could, Fairday managed to grab hold of Margo's foot. Yanking hard, she tried desperately to pull her out. But something was stopping Margo from exiting the mirror. Fairday focused on the reflection and saw that her sister was tugging on something behind the door, something red and sparkling. "Please, God!" she pleaded as she held on to Margo's foot. "Let go, Margo! Let it go!" Her voice rose in fear as she gave one great heave. Margo came flying out of the mirror. Fairday fell backward as her sister tumbled down on top of her.

She lay there, breathing hard, trying to comprehend what had just happened. Margo was all right; Fairday was relieved to hear her rosy giggle. Suddenly, a hard object dropped onto her face. She bolted upright and something fell into her lap. A shoe! Well, not just any shoe—a bright red high-heeled sneaker covered in rubies and diamonds. *This is what I saw in the mirror.* She held it up, taking note of the silky black ribbon tied to the heel.

Margo squirmed and reached out for it. "Where did this come from?" Fairday asked. The sneaker seemed to buzz with electricity, and pulsing vibrations moved through her fingers.

"My shoe, Far-fey? My shoe!" Margo shot out both a question and a statement, pointing to the treasure.

"This is really unbelievable, Margo! How did you get this?" Fairday asked, as though Margo were going to start speaking flawless English and explain how she had come across the extraordinary item. Clearly Margo could see the door in the mirror too!

"My shoe, my shoe, my shoe!" was the response, her tantrum voice growing louder with each declaration.

"Oh, right," she said. At two years old, Margo wasn't likely to see anything unusual about finding a jewel-encrusted high-heeled sneaker behind an invisible door that could only be seen through a mirror's reflection. Nope, nothing at all odd about that! If it hadn't been for the weight of the shoe in her hand, Fairday probably would have thought she was dreaming all this. *What* was going on?

Fairday heard footsteps running down the second-floor hallway, followed by her mother's concerned voice. "Fairday, is everything all right up there?"

Immediately, she stood up and yelled down the stairs, "We're fine, Mom." Fairday then snatched up Margo and the shoe, noticing that the door was no longer in the mirror's reflection. Not wanting to explain anything about what had just happened, she chucked the sneaker into the third-floor room and closed the door. It was just so unimaginable; who would believe her? *Lizzy would,* she thought as she rushed to pull herself together and smoothed out Margo's hair and clothes. Fairday put on a calm face just as Mrs. Morrow appeared in the archway.

"I thought I heard you yelling." Her mother was panting as she looked them both over. "*What* happened?"

Fairday hated to lie, but she also didn't know exactly how to explain that she had almost lost her sister in some crazy mirror, and the yelling had only been her freaking out about it. What would her mother think? After all, she wasn't exactly sure *what* had just happened.

She started to shrug and give a noncommittal reply,

when she was saved by her sister's exclamation of "MA!" Margo reached out for her mother and Fairday handed her over, thinking how lucky it was that anything Margo said would just be chalked up as funny baby prattle.

"Hi, babypoo! How's my little snookiebear? Did you have fun up here with your big sister?" Mrs. Morrow took Margo and snuggled her close. Turning her attention to Fairday, she said, "Honey, I'm concerned. Is there anything you want to tell me?"

"No, I'm fine. Really! I was startled by a spider, that's all."

"Well, if you're sure, then," her mom said, looking skeptical. "You know if you want to talk about anything, I'm here."

Before Fairday could respond, Margo blurted out, "My shoe, Mama. My pretty shoe." Fairday froze.

"Whose shoe, baby? You want one of your shoes? Let's go and get you settled for bed, and you can show me all of your shoes, all right, pumpkin?" Mrs. Morrow kissed Margo's chubby cheek.

"Margo shoes?" Margo's head popped up at the mention of her own stylish selection of pink and purple shoes, and a wide smile spread across her face.

Mrs. Morrow turned to Fairday. "Thanks for watching her, honey. It's almost time for you to start getting ready for bed too. You'll want to be well rested for your weekend with Lizzy tomorrow after school. I'm sure you girls will be up half the night poking around this place." She turned to leave with Margo slung over her shoulder.

Fairday turned her attention to the mirror. It appeared to be functioning normally, with just her reflection looking back. Tentatively, she reached out and touched the surface. It was solid; her fingers brushed lightly over the smooth glass. She was now certain that someone or something was sharing this house with her family. Whatever or whoever it was had just attempted to steal her baby sister! Feeling scared, she stepped away from it. The thought of a stranger creeping around was very disturbing, but she couldn't help feeling somewhat intrigued by the mystery of it all. Noticing the sheet her father had previously removed lying on the floor, she picked it up and threw it over the mirror, covering it. Perhaps the door couldn't be opened if it was blocked. Though, of course, there was no way to be certain.

Fairday was feeling unsettled, but she determined there was nothing else she could accomplish at the moment. Heeding her mother's advice about getting some rest, she decided to call it a night, and went back into the room to grab the clues and the sneaker. This time when she left, she made sure the door was undeniably closed. As she passed under the archway, an eerie tingle caused goose bumps to spread out over her arms, and she couldn't shake the distinct feeling that this case was really going to put the Detective Mystery Squad to the test. Would they be ready for the challenge?

# ~ ELEVEN ~

## A STARTLING SWITCH

Fairday's eyes flew open almost an hour early on Friday morning. She was tired but couldn't wait for Lizzy to come over after school. Plus, her mind kept replaying last night's wild events. After reviewing the incident with the mirror and trying to figure out the sparkling sneaker, she couldn't make sense of anything. Hopefully whoever had the other shoe wasn't going to be coming back for the one Margo had taken.

Fairday figured there was time to read before heading downstairs to breakfast. Last night she had stayed up late finishing *The Lion, the Witch, and the Wardrobe* but couldn't turn out the light until she knew how everything ended up in Narnia. Not being able to leave a story when the plot picked up probably accounted for the fact that she typically devoured a few books a week. Once Fairday entered the world within the pages, she was lost, and she didn't like coming up for air until she was done.

Not wanting to begin a new story, Fairday decided to read a little of her favorite book, since she already knew how it ended. She walked to her dresser to grab *The Wizard of Oz* and was puzzled to find it wasn't there. The book had been right in front of her jewelry box last night. Noticing a folded piece of paper sitting where her prized possession had been, Fairday picked it up and read it.

*Now we each have something that belongs to the other. You'll get back what's yours when I get back what's mine.*

The handwriting was fancy, but luckily she could read it. There was no signature on the front or the back. Who could have left this message? *Oh my goodness, there was definitely someone in here while I was sleeping!* She shivered at the thought of a stranger in her room. All of the crazy images she had seen and the sounds she had heard since moving into the Begonia House were too much.

Fairday knew what she had to do. There was no way she could wait until tonight to share the events with Lizzy. Someone had been in her bedroom uninvited, and whoever it was had taken one of her favorite items. She needed to talk to her parents; they'd know what to do. Maybe the rumors about the house being haunted weren't gossip at all!

Dashing down the hallway to her parents' room, Fairday felt uneasy. The paintings on the walls loomed above her, making her feel self-conscious. Keeping her head down, she tried to figure out exactly what to say.

The door was ajar. Fairday was reaching out to push it open when she heard her name. Sucking in her breath, she paused, wondering if she should knock and wishing she had the extendable ears from Harry Potter. Instead she found herself leaning in to hear the conversation better, though she typically didn't consider herself a snoop.

Mrs. Morrow's concerned voice came through loud and clear. "I'm really worried about Fairday, honey. I don't know what's going on since we moved here. Maybe I shouldn't have mentioned the rumors about the house being haunted. You and I know they aren't real, but Fairday seems jumpier than usual."

"I don't think you need to worry, dear," Mr. Morrow replied in even tones. "Fairday has always had a great imagination, and I'm sure there's nothing to be concerned about."

"I don't agree. It all started the first day, when she thought she heard bagpipes and there was nothing there."

"True, but this old house is drafty, and the wind coming in through the cracks in the walls could create all kinds of sounds she isn't used to. Nothing to fret over."

"Maybe that first day, but what about last night? Fairday

acted like she heard something on the stairs, and she wouldn't tell me what it was. Pat, you should've seen her face; it was white and she looked like she'd seen a ghost."

Fairday had thought she'd hidden her reaction well, but apparently her mother's intuition was spot on.

"You know all the reading she does. Books can really activate the imagination. I, for one, think it's a good thing!"

"I think it could be more than that. Last night I heard her yelling, and I ran to the third floor. Fairday's excuse was weak, and she was behaving *very* strangely," Mrs. Morrow said. "She said she'd seen a spider, but she's never been afraid of them, so I find it hard to believe that seeing one would cause the ruckus she created."

Fairday was listening silently, afraid to make a sound. Her mom thought she was losing it. Showing them the note now would be another point against her.

"Pru, we know Fairday was apprehensive about the move. I'm sure her nerves are close to the surface with all the changes in her life. She's fine, really. Plus, Lizzy will be visiting this weekend, and I'm sure that will take the edge off." Mr. Morrow's steady disposition came through. Fairday was happy to know that at least one of her parents didn't think she was insane.

Backing away from the door, she made her way stealthily to her room. Clutching the note in her hand, she knew the only person she would be able to share her thoughts with was Lizzy. Her best friend wouldn't think she was mental. But was it a good idea to keep something this big to herself? What if their lives were in danger? Concentrating at school wasn't going to be easy while she worried about an intruder traipsing around her new home.

# TWELVE

## THE DMS REUNITED

The daylight began to fade, painting the sky with long pink-ish purple streaks of color. Fairday's bedroom was hazy with the last dusty beams shining through the window. As she closed the door and switched on the overhead lamp, shadows shifted over the walls. Lizzy flung her overnight bag in the corner, then sat down on the bed, listening with rapt attention to Fairday's recount of the incident involving Margo going through the mirror. Fairday left out the part about the high-heeled sneaker, intending to present that incredible item when the time was right.

"It was just so crazy! I mean, how did Margo get into that mirror? And where on earth does it go? Anyone else would think I was mental, right?" Fairday shot off these last questions to Lizzy before she finally took a breath.

"Well," Lizzy said, her forehead wrinkling in thought as she tapped her chin, "if you say it happened, I believe you. I'm not sure how, but I know we'll figure it out. I think it's time to check out all the stuff you found. Maybe that will give us some answers, or at least point us in the right direction." She pulled off her DMS pack and laid it in her lap. Within moments, all of her detective tools were sprawled out on the bed. There was the digital camera, the binoculars and headlamp, her brother's multitool key chain, and something else Fairday noticed: a pair of tweezers.

"Very useful," Lizzy explained. "They belonged to my mom. She used them for eyebrow plucking and was going to toss them. But I rescued them from the trash. They're great for picking up small things. I can't believe we didn't already have a pair. It seems so obvious. Duh, right?" Her face screwing up into a funny expression, Lizzy grasped the tweezers and pinched the air with them a few times.

"Okay, then, let's get on with it." Fairday took a deep breath, agreeing with the suggestion to start the case by examining all the clues she had collected. Last night she had put them into her bag to show them to Lizzy like a magician pulling a rabbit out of a hat. Her notepad was on the floor next to her, already flipped to the correct page, and the pen was at the ready to record any ingenious thoughts that might pop into their heads. In the center of the room, Fairday stood with her DMS pack at her feet, feeling like an actress onstage preparing for opening night. Bending down, she unzipped it, thankful Lizzy was finally here. Hopefully more pieces of the puzzle would click into place.

The first item she pulled out of the pack was the silver hairbrush, which she handed to her friend. "Here's the brush I told you about." Fairday's breath came out in a rush as Lizzy began turning it over, carefully observing every inch of it. She picked up the magnifying glass and began her examination. "If you look closely, you'll see the initials," Fairday instructed, and Lizzy quickly found them. She zoomed in and scrutinized the engraving.

"Wow, this seems pretty old. No one has hairbrushes like this anymore. My grandma has one like it on her dressing table," Lizzy noted. Moving the hand lens over the bristles, she picked up her tweezers and used them to pull out a dull, reddish strand of hair. "Check this out! It might not be much, but I think we should bag and label it so we can look at it later and see if it ties in to anything else we uncover." The ziplock bags were in a box Fairday had swiped from the kitchen; detectives needed clear, clean containers to keep their clues in. She opened one, and Lizzy slipped the strand of hair into it, marking it with a Sharpie: HAIR FROM BRUSH.

"Oh my gosh, I didn't even see that!" Fairday exclaimed, wondering how she could have missed such a thing and doubly glad she had her partner here. "Now that you've uncovered the hair, wait until you see this next item." She produced the picture frame with flourish. Fairday handed it over and went back to her notebook to scribble an additional note.

Silver hairbrush with the initials RB
engraved on the back—*red hair in bristles

Lizzy was all business as she pulled the photo closer. "Didn't you say there was some type of writing on the back of this picture?" she asked as she flipped the frame over and began sliding the back out.

"Yeah, but first look at the front and tell me what you think," Fairday said.

Once Lizzy had the picture out of the frame, she studied it. "Hmm, the hair might be from her, right?" she said, raising her eyebrows.

"That's what I was thinking," Fairday replied. "And look at her finger. Is it me or does it seem like she's pointing at something?"

Lizzy looked back at the photo, then slowly moved her own hand to mimic the image frozen in time. "Yes, definitely! But what?"

"I'm not sure, but it might be a clue. Do you see anything else that looks important?" Fairday asked. Two heads were better than one, and who knew what else her friend would find?

Lizzy moved the magnifying glass slowly along the front

of the picture. Not finding anything more of interest, she turned it over and began examining the back, specifically along the bottom edge, noticing the faint markings. Her eye moved closer to the lens, trying to get a better idea of what was written. "I can't make this out, but it does say something. Let me snap a picture of it so I can put it on the computer and play around with it later," she said, whipping the camera out of its case and zooming in on the inscription. The flash of bright light burst through the room. "Got it! Hopefully I can enhance it. Maybe we'll get lucky and have something to work with."

Fairday nodded in agreement as she dug back down into her bag. Her fingers found the brass key. "Look at this!" she said. "I don't know what in the world it opens, but it was on a dresser in the third-floor room, and it looks just like the key to the front gate of this house."

"It does look important and unique," Lizzy remarked. "Have you looked around for any locks it might fit? What about the dresser you mentioned or maybe an old trunk?" Her mind raced with ideas.

"So far I've been flummoxed! Of course, this house has so many items that I'm sure there are tons of possibilities I haven't explored yet," Fairday said. "Maybe we can make a list of places to check and work systematically until we find the correct lock?"

"That's a great idea. Have you found anything else?" Lizzy said with interest, handing the key back to Fairday.

"Yes! I found this old hourglass, and the sand doesn't move. What do you think?"

Taking the hourglass from Fairday's outstretched hand, Lizzy began shaking it. She then strapped the headlamp on and used the magnifying glass to look at the sparkling sand up close. "The path is clear. I have no idea why it isn't working," she said, handing it back to Fairday. "We'll have to look at it again later. What else have you got?"

"Well, this morning my *Wizard of Oz* book was missing, and I found this note in its place."

Lizzy grabbed the slip of paper and read it. "That's totally creepy! Are you thinking it might be who you saw in the mirror?"

"Who else could've left it, right? After overhearing my parents discussing my mental state, I know it wasn't them."

"True. This case keeps getting trickier by the minute. Is that everything?"

"Nope. I've saved the best for last! Drum roll, please," Fairday said, her excitement heightening as she reached into her DMS pack one last time. "Wait until you see this!" She grasped the heel of the sneaker and pulled it out. It glimmered brilliantly in her hand, sparkling red with iridescent rainbows; the silky black ribbon dangled over her wrist.

"Wow!" Lizzy said in awe, looking stunned as the sneaker shimmered in the dusty light. Fairday handed it over, and Lizzy held it cautiously. "This really is amazing!" She set the sneaker down on the bed and watched it intently, as if it were going to disappear any minute or had never been there to begin with.

"That's what Margo pulled out of the mirror. And I think someone was wearing it at the time. Totally freaky." She shrugged, her expression filled with bewilderment.

"Totally freaky is right." Lizzy picked up the sneaker again. "I mean, who ever heard of high-heeled sneakers? I've never seen anything like this when I've been shoe shopping with my mom. And what's with all the jewels? It has to be something magical. I can feel a weird vibration when I'm holding it." She set it down again. "I wonder what it can do. It's a really pretty sneaker," she said. "Have you tried it on yet?"

"No, not yet. I felt the vibrations, too, and I think you're right—there's definitely something supernatural about that sneaker. It's so strange to think there could be someone in this house with the other shoe," Fairday said, biting her lip.

"Let's do it, then. Let's each try it on. You go first, since you found it," Lizzy said. She bounced off the bed, snatched up the sneaker, and thrust it at Fairday.

"Um, all right." Fairday sat down on the bed. "Okay, here goes." She untied the laces and leaned over, rushing to pull off her left shoe. Fairday's attempt at trying on the sneaker proved disappointing, as it was much too small. "Ah, well. It's clearly not going to fit me. You try it on." She handed it back to Lizzy.

Lizzy sat next to her and took off her own shoe. Sliding

the high-heeled sneaker onto her foot, she exclaimed, "It fits! I can't believe it!" Fairday watched as Lizzy stood up and spun around, modeling the strange footwear. It was almost as if it had been crafted for her, which seemed appropriate because her friend couldn't resist dazzling things.

"My foot feels so weird! Like it's pulsating," Lizzy stated, propping her foot up on the bed and reaching down to touch the red rubies, shining diamonds, and silky ribbon. "We definitely have to find the other one and figure out how to get into that mirror!" she said, taking off the sneaker.

"You're probably right," Fairday replied, twisting the end of her ponytail. "I'm not all that comfortable with the idea of someone sneaking around this place, looking for their stolen shoe. Margo's thievery might have made them angry."

"You betcha! Let's head up to the third-floor room. I think it's time to shift this investigation into full swing and figure out exactly who or what is creeping around this house," Lizzy said as she got up and began lining up the items one by one on the dresser. "I mean, I would prefer we find whoever it is, rather than have them find us." She zoomed in with her camera and clicked pictures of the brush, the bag with the hair in it, the photo, the key, the hourglass, and the high-heeled sneaker. She then sealed the camera back into its case and began to gather her detective tools. As she repacked them, she added, "That would not be good."

Fairday thought about Lizzy's statement and heard Dif's voice echoing in her head. *See any dead people yet?* At the time, she'd thought it was a stupid question, coming from a stupid boy who meant to embarrass her. But now she felt like it could really happen. Would they actually meet up with a ghost? Fairday's stomach bubbled in anxiety. She knew they needed to find out what was going on in her house, but this investigation was getting scarier by the minute! What if they came face to face with the mystery person haunting her house? She needed to remain calm. Her best friend would be right beside her. They would protect each other.

Fairday stuffed all the clues back into her bag, along with the notebook and pen. Both girls took a deep breath, looked at each other anxiously, and then headed out to begin their investigation of the Begonia House.

# THIRTEEN

## AN UNPREDICTABLE SITUATION

Lizzy stared into the mirror and tentatively touched the glass. "I can't imagine sticking my hand through here. It must have been unbelievable!" she said, stepping back and looking at Fairday.

"It was. I can't even explain what was going through my head. When my mom heard me yell and came running up, I just played it off like nothing had happened. I mean, what could I have possibly said? 'Oh, by the way, Mom, Margo pulled this sneaker out of a door that I thought I saw inside this mirror, which has just disappeared. Sorry you missed it'? She'd have me institutionalized!" Fairday moved closer to the mirror and peered into it.

"Well, I think we should start by setting up a clean area

and then poke around to see what more we can uncover. We definitely have to find the lock that fits that key. . . ." Lizzy's voice trailed off as she glanced to the left and noticed the barricaded door that led to the balcony. "What on earth is that?" she asked.

"Ah! Yes, you know my dad. That door leads out to an old balcony. Dad couldn't find the key to lock it, so he put up the yellow police tape to emphasize that he doesn't want us to go out there." Fairday smiled, adding, "He may have gone a little overboard." She gestured to the crisscross pattern that covered the entire door.

"Jeez, he must have used the whole roll of tape." Lizzy laughed, flipping her blond curls. "Well, I guess that's one area we don't need to worry about. Though . . ." She hesitated, her blue eyes glinting mischievously. "We should probably check to see if the brass key fits the lock on this door." She looked at Fairday, nodding. "Just to rule it out."

Fairday thought about it for a moment. She hated to disobey her father, but Lizzy was right. In order to conduct this investigation properly, they would have to check everything. And besides, they didn't have to walk out onto the balcony. "I agree," Fairday answered, and bent down to unzip her DMS pack. She reached in and fumbled around for the key. "All right, here we go." Walking over to the door, she pulled back the caution tape, looked down the staircase to make sure her dad wasn't coming, then stuck the key into the lock. She turned it to the right and the lock clicked. "Wow, that was easy!" Fairday said in amazement, then turned it back to unlock it. "I can't believe it fits." She slowly swung open the door and revealed the balcony to Lizzy.

The strong, cool autumn air smacked them both in the face. They remained behind the threshold of the door, gripping the sides as they leaned over and watched the balcony sway dangerously. The wind suddenly began to rise, causing the boards to creak and groan as they shifted. "Look at that!" Lizzy shouted.

Fairday followed Lizzy's pointing finger and saw what had caught her friend's attention. The weeping willow was glowing. Twinkling bluish leaves were springing up one after the other all along the barren branches. The whole tree seemed to be lifting its limbs and extending them toward the balcony. The rushing wind whipped their hair, making the girls look like they were about to take flight. It sounded as if a tornado were touching down right in front of them.

"SHUT THE DOOR!" Lizzy screamed above the howling gale. They both took a step back and Fairday turned around to grab hold of the doorknob, then froze.

"Lizzy! Look," she said in a forceful whisper. Lizzy turned, and her jaw dropped. Time stopped as the two stared into the mirror. There stood a lady. She beckoned them from behind the glass, her green eyes flashing, her fiery red hair static with electricity. Fairday felt something wrap around her ankle and tore her gaze from the reflection to look down. A glowing willow branch had ensnared her leg and was tightening its grip. "AH!" she yelled, grabbing the door and slamming it as hard as she could, snapping the branch in two. Fairday bent down and yanked it off her leg. Almost instantaneously, she looked back at the mirror and saw the woman was gone.

"WHAT WAS THAT?" Lizzy was still yelling but clearly trying to get ahold of herself. She leaned against the wall, panting in terror.

"I don't know! This is nuts!" Fairday said. Chewing on her thumbnail, she continued. "Who is that lady, and how did the tree come alive? It tried to grab me!" She reached down and snatched the broken branch from the floor, then snapped it in half. It was brittle and dried, with no leaves . . . a dead stick. Hearts racing, the girls looked at each other, barely breathing as they listened to make sure the commotion hadn't alerted Mr. and Mrs. Morrow to their rule-breaking. Silence met them, and then the sudden ringing of a phone broke the spell.

"This is serious. That lady, whoever she is, does not look friendly," Lizzy said, walking to the mirror and picking up the sheet. "I think it's best to cover this. I mean, maybe you're right, and she can't come through if it's blocked." She threw the sheet into the air. It fanned out and floated down over the ornate mirror, once again concealing its glass. "Let's follow through with our plan to search the secret room and see if we can find any more clues that might lead us in the right direction. We need to know what we're dealing with. You know my motto—'Knowledge is power!'" Lizzy proclaimed, putting on a brave face.

"Yeah, that's the best thing to do," Fairday replied, feeling shaken. She snatched up her DMS pack; took a deep, calming breath; and opened the door across the hall to the third-floor room.

# ~ℱℴURTEEN~

## MORE THAN MEETS THE EYE

The two girls cleared out a spot and set up their station. Taking the picture frame out of her DMS pack, Fairday flinched as she stared into the green eyes of the red-haired lady. The face they had just seen in the mirror was terrifying, not at all like this pretty woman. Did those eyes just move? She shifted her gaze away for just a second, then snapped her stare back. Nothing was different. Maybe it was just her imagination going berserk. This week had not been easy on her nerves.

Once everything was in place, they began to move about the room. Fairday nudged Lizzy and pointed to the bagpipe stuffed in the corner. Lizzy walked toward it, and the spiders, as if on cue, all scuttled away, causing her to step back. Fairday heard a murmur that sounded something like *yuck*, followed by a disgusted snort. Lizzy pressed on, bending down to get a better look at the mouthpiece with the magnifying glass. She examined the moldy, cracked reed. "This thing is revolting," she said.

"That's an excellent word for it," Fairday commented over her shoulder as she turned and walked over to the wardrobe. Running her fingers along the scratched wood, she jiggled the front door handles, which were made of iron and shaped like two claws clasped together. It was locked, though there seemed to be no lock in sight. She moved to the right side, pushing it out from the wall a few inches, and peeked around the back.

"Whoa! Lizzy, come and look at this!" Fairday shouted.

"What?" Lizzy disregarded the sticky bagpipe and hastened over to where she stood.

Fairday moved to the side and motioned to the back of the wardrobe. "Back here—take a look."

Lizzy moved into her spot and leaned in to see what had caught her friend's eye. "There's writing on this!" she said. "I can't read it, though. I need the flashlight."

Fairday raced over to her DMS pack and pulled out the flashlight. Then she and Lizzy pushed the clunky piece of furniture out as far as they could. "What do you think that means?" Fairday asked as she illuminated the words etched into the center of the back panel. They were written in the same fancy letters as the initials *RB* on the hairbrush. They read:

*KNOCK THRICE AND THREE*
*TO OPEN THE DOOR.*
*KNOCK THRICE AND FOUR*
*TO LOCK IT ONCE MORE.*

"They're instructions," Lizzy said as both girls slid out from behind the wardrobe. "Knock three times and then three more to open the door, and then three times plus four to lock it again." Fairday knew she was right, remembering that *thrice* meant something in threes. *So that explains why there's no actual lock on it,* she thought.

Lizzy stood in front of the wardrobe, poised to knock, but then stopped. "Maybe you should write that down so we don't forget how to lock the door." She shot Fairday a furtive glance, adding, "I mean, just in case something crazy happens."

Fairday had her notebook and pen in hand before Lizzy even finished her thought. "Got it." She flipped the notebook closed and shoved it into her back pocket.

Lizzy knocked on the door: one, two, three. She paused, and then one, two, three, again. The clawlike handles unclenched, releasing their grip on each other. Both girls held their breath as Lizzy swung open the door to reveal its hidden contents, which were instantly disappointing.

"Two wire hangers! That's it?" Lizzy said, throwing her hands up in disbelief. The hangers rocked back and forth on a bar that ran along the inside.

"Ah, well." Fairday shrugged. "It's pretty cool how it opens and locks. I wonder how that works." She turned to look at Lizzy. "What do you think?"

"I think it's probably just a freaky piece of furniture," Lizzy answered, sounding somewhat disenchanted. She held the doors shut with one hand, paused for effect, and then, with the other, knocked three times plus four. The claw fingers once again closed tightly onto one another, mysteriously locking up the wardrobe. Lizzy turned to face Fairday as she added, "You're right, though, that is pretty cool. Plus, we can use it to store some of our secret DMS stuff. Keep anything important away from Margo's sticky fingers and Auntie Em's drool." She grinned and then headed toward a stack of yellowing newspapers toppling over in a corner of the room.

Fairday stared at the extravagant wardrobe with its ancient-looking wood and iron claws. She wanted to try the door, too, even though she knew there was nothing in it. She knocked three times and then three more, and the claws unclasped. Peering inside, Fairday banged on the back, then ran her hands along the inside, shining the flashlight all around the interior. A thin red string sticking out of a back corner caught her eye. Reaching up, she pinched it between her fingers and pulled. A panel swung open and she ducked just in time to avoid being hit by a falling object. It was a book.

Fairday picked it up and flipped through the pages. "Lizzy, come quick. You won't believe it. I think I found a diary!"

"Does it say whose it is?" Lizzy asked, hurrying over to Fairday's side.

Fairday's eyes quickly scanned to the bottom of the page. "Well, this entry is signed Ruby. Maybe that's the *R* in the initials *RB* from the brush . . . Ruby Begonia?"

# ~❧ FIFTEEN ❧~

## TALES FROM THE PAST

Fairday and Lizzy stared at the diary. The worn cover looked as though it were bruised, and its yellowing pages, with sections missing, gave them the impression that it was very old.

As Fairday handed it to Lizzy, a dried red rose petal fell from between the pages. It crumbled a bit as it landed on the floor. Lizzy carefully picked up the delicate flower with the tweezers.

"Oh my goodness! That looks just like the ones I found the day Margo went into the mirror!" Fairday said. "I wonder where they're coming from."

"Jot it down in your notebook," Lizzy replied, excitement edging into her voice as she put the petal aside so they could bag and label it.

*Diary found in secret panel of
wardrobe—dried rose petal inside.*

Fairday considered the book in her hand for a moment. "It feels weird to be looking through someone else's diary," she worried.

"I know, but we definitely should. I mean, who knows what secrets are written in there."

"I guess. But I wouldn't want strangers reading my diary, even if I wasn't around to know about it," Fairday added.

"Me neither," Lizzy replied. "But there are mysterious things happening here, and this could give us some clues we need." She smiled mischievously. "It's fine, Fairday. Really!"

Fairday shrugged. "You're right. Let's see what it has to say!"

Sitting on the floor, the girls each held part of the diary as they began deciphering the small handwriting.

*October 28, 1949*

*My Dearest Diary—*

*You are my favorite birthday present this year! My father gave you to me and said I might want to start recording my adventures now that I'm eleven years old. Oh! I do hope to have many adventures. I want to see the world!*

Lizzy paused, looking up incredulously at Fairday. "I don't believe it! She was our age when she wrote this!"

"I know!" Fairday said, squinting at the page.

I live in a big house in Ashpot, Connecticut, with my father. My mother died the day I was born, so I never knew her. I wish I remembered her. I have a picture, and she was very pretty. She had deep brown eyes and long brown hair. I don't look like her at all. I have bright red hair and green eyes. My father says I look like his mother, but I don't think so. I'm not sure who I'm like. I feel different from everyone around here.

I don't want to bore you by being gloomy, so I'll write more later, but I hope you know how delighted I am to have someone to tell my secrets to!       ~Ruby

Flipping through the early entries, they noticed most of them were short, with simple facts about Ruby and her daily life. She did seem lonely, Fairday thought. Coming to a long entry, they stopped to read.

April 5, 1950

Diary Dearest—

I still can't believe what happened today. Maybe writing it down will help me figure things out. I was playing the bagpipes for my father outside his study, when suddenly there was a knock at the front door. I stopped to watch as our maid answered. Standing in the entrance was an old, scruffy woman. I thought for sure Father would turn her away, but she was welcomed in, as if she were an expected guest!

I ran down the stairs, hiding in my best spying spot under the grand staircase. I crept out just after Father walked into the sitting room and shut the door. Opening it a crack, I heard him shouting about my mother's death. He mentioned something about blueprints, yelling that a promise had not been delivered. I was scared! I've never heard my father so infuriated. His voice was shaking as he swore he'd never pay the woman, that he never wanted to see her ugly face haunting his doorstep again. I watched as the woman sat quietly while he raged on and on. Then he threw something small and shiny that landed at her feet.

It was a brass key. The lady began to laugh and told him she would have her revenge if he didn't pay. I raced into the kitchen just as my father came out and stormed up the stairs. I was frightened, but I had to know more about this visitor. What had she done to make my father so angry? Why had he thrown a key at her? I looked back into the room and the woman, whom I heard him call Eldrich, was still sitting on the sofa with a sinister smile. Only now, it was directed at me. She lifted up the hem of her skirt, and on her feet were the most dazzling sneakers I have ever seen! They had diamonds and rubies all over them! I was mesmerized by their brilliance and struggled to look away. Our eyes met, and she winked at me. The maid then noticed I was in the doorway and hurried to send me upstairs. I obeyed, but as I reached the top step, I turned to get one last look at the woman. She spun around, raising her hands above her head, and recited a riddle. I couldn't quite hear, but it sounded like she said something about the blueprints. Then, laughing hysterically, she turned and disappeared from view.

Later, when I went back to the sitting room, the brass key was still lying on the floor, and I took it. The only thing I know about it is that Father always said he wore it to remind himself of his failings. What that means, I don't know. I rubbed it with my fingers, trying to read its energy. Why did my father think he had failed? And what did the key have to do with my mother?　　　~Ruby

Fairday and Lizzy looked at each other. "So the shoes belong to the gypsy-looking woman? Is that who we saw in the mirror? Or could it be Ruby?" Fairday asked, her nerves jumping at the thought.

"Wow! I can't believe we found out about the sneaker. I'm not sure who has the other one in the mirror. Maybe it *is* the gypsy," Lizzy said.

"Could be," Fairday replied, her heart pounding in her chest. "But now we do know that Ruby played the bagpipes. I wonder if she ever figured out what the key was for. Let's see what else we can piece together." Focusing on the next entry, they read:

June 21, 1950

Dearest Diary,

You'll never believe what I found tonight! I was searching my father's room looking for more clues about my
mother, when I came across an old trunk. It was locked,
but there was a hole in the side, and I was able to get
my fingers through. I pulled out a silver canister that
contained a set of blueprints. I think these were what my
father was talking to Eldrich about! There are drawings
of every room in this house with odd rhymes all around
the pages. And listen to this, when I tried one, it worked!
I moved a wall! It's a little scary, but I'm excited to
see what else these can do. Finally I get to have a real
adventure! Just like my father when he was traveling the
world, collecting treasures. Who knows what magic I'll
discover. I can't wait to try more of them out. But for
now the canister is tucked away so my father won't find
out I have it                                          ~Ruby

Fairday remembered the walls that seemed to move.
Had that been her imagination or did she accidentally say
a rhyme from the blueprints? "Um, Lizzy, I didn't mention
this because I wasn't sure if anything had even happened,
but when I was exploring the third-floor room one day, I
thought I saw the wall move."

"Do you know what you said?"

"Not exactly. It could have been anything." Fairday shivered with the knowledge that her words could hold more power than she ever expected.

"Well, maybe if you remember, we can try it out," Lizzy said, pointing to the next entry.

*September 19, 1950*

*Dearest Diary,*

*Everything is ruined! Tonight my father found out I had the blueprints. He was very angry and took them away. Thank goodness I learned the magic of this house and I no longer need them. I know if he ever sees me with them again I'll be grounded until I'm an old woman. I don't plan to look for them.          ~Ruby*

"So that's it? The entries just stop?" Lizzy said with a hint of frustration. "I wonder why the pages at the end are missing."

"I don't know," Fairday said as she wrote down the clues from Ruby's diary in her notebook. "But I'm sure glad we found this, and that at least most of the pages are here."

Magical blueprints with rhymes, hidden somewhere. Where could they be?

Is the brass key the one Thurston Begonia threw at the gypsy? Why did he

wear it around his neck? Did Ruby ever
figure out what it unlocked? Key we
found unlocks balcony—and willow comes
alive.

Shoes belonged to Eldrich, so how did they
end up inside the mirror? Who's in the
mirror? Gypsy or Ruby?

Lizzy leaned over Fairday's shoulder to scan the list, then
nodded. "Looks like you got everything. Why don't you
pack up the new clues and I'll go back and finish looking
through those newspapers."

"Okay, sounds good." Taking the ziplock baggies out of
her pack, Fairday labeled the rose petal and the diary, then
placed them inside her bag with the other evidence.

# ∾ SIXTEEN ⟊

## LIZZY'S FIND

Lizzy's voice rang out from across the room. "Fairday! I found the red-haired lady's name!" She was kneeling next to the newspapers, shaking one of the pages above her head. Fairday hurried over and dropped down beside her. Lizzy spread out the front page of the *Ashpot Weekly* in front of them. The newspaper was dated October 16, 1958, and even though it was torn off at the top and bottom, most of the article was legible. "Here, look," Lizzy said, pointing at the headline. In a rushed voice, she read:

## THE MISSING BRIDE

The picture underneath the story was in black-and-white, but Fairday was certain it was the red-haired lady. With her heart banging against her chest, she listened as Lizzy read:

Ruby Begonia, only daughter of the well-known world adventurer Thurston Begonia, went missing yesterday. Officers were called to the Begonia House shortly after 3:00 p.m. after having been notified that the bride-to-be could not be found. Miss Begonia was set to marry Gilford Pomfrey at a 3:30 p.m. ceremony taking place at the exclusive manor. She was last seen just before 3:00 p.m. in one of the upstairs rooms of the home, where she had been having her portrait photographed as a gift for her father. Harold Frogtrom, the artist commissioned to do the work, was the last person to see Miss Begonia that day. Mr. Frogtrom stated, "She was just fine—cheerful, and looking forward to getting married. I left the room so she could change into her wedding dress, and I went downstairs. That's all I know." Investigators are continuing to question everyone who was present during this mysterious disappearance but still have no clues as to what may have happened to the bride.

"That has to be her!" Lizzy exclaimed, dropping the paper and looking at Fairday. "Ruby Begonia, *RB*, like on the brush and in the diary!"

"I know!" Fairday replied. "The photo in the paper looks the same as the one in the frame. I'm glad you looked through these old newspapers. Who knew they would be so important!" Glancing over at her friend, she noticed Lizzy scrutinizing something. "What's up?" she asked.

Lizzy looked from the article to a spot in the room. "Not only is it the same picture, but if I'm not mistaken, this photo was taken right over there," she said. "Ruby Begonia's sitting in *that* chair in the picture." She pointed over to the chair in the corner. "It has the same striped pattern." Lizzy grabbed the frame off the table and held it up.

Fairday looked from the photo in the newspaper to the picture in the frame and then to the chair. Each hair on her arm stood up. Suddenly, she blurted out, "Lizzy, I forgot to tell you! The clock on the kitchen stove is stopped at exactly three o'clock. I wrote it down." She flipped through the pages of her notebook and handed it over.

Lizzy read over Fairday's notes. "It can't be a coincidence. I mean, the article says she disappeared sometime around three in the afternoon." Lizzy moved toward the chair and touched its cushion. "Which means Ruby Begonia was right *here* just before she vanished!" Someone called out from below, breaking the hushed spell that had momentarily fallen over them, and they both looked toward the door.

"Ten o'clock, girls! Time to get ready for bed." It was Mr. Morrow. They heard footsteps climbing the staircase, and then his head popped through the door. "So," he said, peering around the room. "What sort of fascinating secrets have we found up here?"

Fairday blandly answered, "Hi, Dad. Not too much, just a bunch of junk, pretty much." She knew she had to play it cool, because her parents were already suspicious that something was up.

Lizzy grabbed the article and slipped it into her DMS pack. "Neat place, though, Mr. Morrow. It'll be a great bed-and-breakfast when it's finished." She slung her pack over her shoulder and walked out of the room. Fairday followed close behind. She quickly glanced toward the mirror, making sure it was covered, and headed down the steps.

# SEVENTEEN

## SHIFTING SHADOWS

The digital face of Fairday's alarm clock proclaimed midnight just as she finished rereading the newspaper article in a whisper. Both girls were huddled on the floor of Fairday's room, hidden underneath a purple comforter with the flashlight propped up on a pillow, illuminating the tentlike area.

"So we know for sure the red-haired lady in the picture is Ruby Begonia. She disappeared on the day of her wedding sometime around three o'clock, and the last place she was seen was the third-floor room," Lizzy calculated, raising her fingers one at a time as she went through the facts.

"Right," Fairday replied, nodding in agreement. "We also know there are probably magical blueprints hidden somewhere around here and that the high-heeled sneakers belong to a gypsy named Eldrich. Plus, we know the brass key somehow activates the willow tree."

"We still need to figure out the hourglass," Lizzy said.

Fairday took it out of her DMS pack and placed it on the floor between them. She shined the flashlight on the hourglass and they considered the strange object. It still wasn't working. As Lizzy put her hand out to give it a shake, sparkling red sand suddenly began to fall. The girls looked at each other with their mouths dropped open.

"How did that happen?" Fairday asked.

"I don't know, but the sand is fascinating. Doesn't it seem to be falling slowly?"

"It does. Weird!"

"Should we pick it up?"

"No, let's just watch it for a while and see what happens. Plus, we still need to go over the interview questions for Larry Lovell."

Fairday dug her project folder out from the folds of her sun-and-moon sleeping bag, along with a piece of paper that listed all the questions she and Lizzy had written down to ask during the interview. Grabbing her pen, she stuck one end into the corner of her mouth and gazed up contemplatively.

"How should we word the questions about Ruby Begonia? I don't want to let on that we actually saw her, or her ghost, or whatever we saw in the mirror. He'll think I'm completely gaga." Fairday stuck out her tongue and rolled her eyes. Lizzy giggled, covering her mouth. "Shhhh," Fairday murmured. "My mom will kill us if we get caught up at this hour."

Lizzy got ahold of herself. Thoughtfully, she suggested, "Well, you could just show him the article and ask if he knows anything about it. You said he worked for the town paper a long time ago, and it wouldn't seem suspicious that you found it in the house and are curious. Which, if you think about it, really is the truth. Just not all of it." She flipped her hair, adding, "Who knows, maybe he wrote it? Too bad the reporter's name was ripped off."

"True," Fairday said. "Should I show him the diary?"

"I don't think so. Let's keep that piece of evidence to ourselves for now."

Fairday slipped the piece of paper back into the folder and closed it, tossing it aside. "Well, we definitely have our work cut out for us, that's for sure."

"You betcha!" Lizzy said.

Just then, the girls heard the floorboards creak right outside their fort. Grabbing each other's arms, their eyes widened as they inched closer together. A looming shadow crossed over the tent, causing fear to rise in Fairday's throat. Neither girl spoke as their hearts beat wildly. They watched the eerie shadow slink back and disappear.

"Is it safe?" Lizzy mouthed.

"I don't know," Fairday whispered. "What should we do?"

Lizzy leaned over and pulled back the tent door to have a look.

"Do you see anything?" Fairday asked, her voice shaking.

"No, but your bedroom door is open," Lizzy said.

"What? I know we definitely closed it! Someone was in here with us! This is just like the night I first moved in. I could've sworn I saw someone standing at the end of my bed. And the door was open then too," Fairday said, pulling her sleeping bag in closer. "You don't think it was the lady from the mirror, do you?"

"Could be or maybe it was your parents checking in on us," Lizzy said. "We should turn on a light to make sure everything is okay."

"No way! I'm not going out there."

"We'll do it together," Lizzy said, grabbing Fairday's hand. Both girls ran out of the fort and switched on the lamp. Their eyes scanned the room, but no one was there.

"I think we should close the door and prop my desk chair against it to keep intruders out," Fairday said, closing her bedroom door as quietly as possible.

"Good idea," Lizzy said, picking up the chair and positioning it under the doorknob. "At least we've set a trap in case someone tries to sneak in."

The girls hurried back into the tent and snuggled deep into their sleeping bags. "We should probably try and get some sleep so we aren't tired. 'Got to have a sharp mind on the morrow!'" Fairday proclaimed in a whisper, dramatically pointing her finger in the air. Humor was the only way she could get over this disturbing experience.

"You betcha! Your father's favorite quote," Lizzy said, her eyes already closed as she added through a yawn, "Night. See you in the morning."

Fairday loved that Lizzy was probably the only other person in the world who appreciated her dad's somewhat strange humor. "Night," she said, wishing sleep came as easily to her as it did to her friend. Shifting her gaze to the falling sand in the hourglass, she watched it until her eyes closed. Wild images circled madly behind her eyelids. And as she fell deeper and deeper into sleep, they spun themselves into the web of her dreams.

Fairday's alarm sounded earlier than usual for a Saturday morning. Stretching, she reached through the opening in the makeshift tent to shut it off. As she pulled her hand back, her eyes fell on the hourglass. The sand had stopped falling. Fairday gently picked it up and flipped it over. Nothing. *Hmm, that's odd,* she thought. *Why did it work last night?* Lizzy was still sleeping soundly, so Fairday poked her lightly on the shoulder.

"Lizzy, wake up!"

"What is it?" Lizzy replied, yawning.

"Look at this! The sand stopped moving." Shaking it, Fairday turned it over again. Still nothing.

"That's totally weird," Lizzy said. "What could've made it stop?"

"I have no idea! But it must mean something, right?"

"I'm sure it does. Could it have anything to do with that creepy shadow we saw last night?"

Fairday shivered at the memory. "It might. We'll have to try to figure it out when we get back from the library."

# EIGHTEEN

## FACT OR FICTION?

*"Ding-dong! Witch is dead. Old witch? Wicked Witch! Ding-dong! Wicked Witch is dead!"* Margo belted out the lyrics to *The Wizard of Oz* sound track that was playing in the Morrow family cruiser.

"Wow, she really gets into the music, doesn't she?" Lizzy said.

"This is her favorite song," Fairday replied, smiling, as the car pulled up in front of the library.

"How fitting," Lizzy murmured, glancing at Fairday.

"She's on her way to becoming the next pop sensation, aren't you, my little snookykins?" Mrs. Morrow piped up proudly, looking back at Margo, who was still bopping to the beat. Her tone became more serious as she addressed

Lizzy and Fairday. "Now, girls, here's my old phone. Fairday, put it in your backpack. I have some errands to run, and then I'll be at the town hall around noon. Lord knows I'll probably be there forever, filling out paperwork for all the permits we're going to need on the house." She rolled her eyes and sighed as she added, "Just call or text me when you're ready to leave."

"Okay, Mom," said Fairday, taking the phone and securing it in a side pocket of her DMS pack. She and Lizzy climbed out of the car and onto the sidewalk. They waved goodbye to Mrs. Morrow as she pulled out into traffic, honked twice, and then disappeared through a green light.

Fairday glanced up at the wide, double-glass doors of the library. An old man, using a cane and sporting a golf cap, was just opening the door. She pulled on the strap of Lizzy's pack. "Hey, do you think that's Larry Lovell?" she asked, nodding toward the doors.

"Could be," Lizzy said as he disappeared into the building. The bell on the clock tower announced with its tenth chime that it was definitely ten o'clock.

It was quiet and cool inside the library. The reception area was just beyond the entranceway. A woman with blond hair was bent over reading some forms at the desk. As Fairday and Lizzy approached, she looked up and smiled at them.

"Hi, girls. Is there something I can help you with?" she asked in a quiet voice.

"Hi, um yes, actually," Fairday replied. "We're meeting Larry Lovell. You wouldn't happen to know if he's here, would you?"

"Larry? Oh yes!" she said. "Mr. Lovell is always here on Saturdays. Just about everyone knows him. He mostly keeps to himself, though." She pointed to a table in the corner of the room. "That's him, over there."

"Thanks!" Fairday said. The girls turned to face each other. "Here's my library card. You'll need it to get on the computer."

"All right, thanks," Lizzy said, taking the card and stuffing it into her pocket. "You go ahead and get started with the interview. I'm going to try and decipher the writing on the back of the photo from the picture I took. If I have time, I'll see if I can find any more stories on the house. You have all the questions we came up with and the article, right?"

"I do," Fairday said, checking the contents of the folder she had just pulled out. "Good luck with the picture and research. I'll come and get you when we're finished." Lizzy traipsed off to find a vacant computer as Fairday turned toward Larry Lovell.

Butterflies fluttered around in her stomach as she approached the old man. He was not very friendly-looking, Fairday discerned. Actually, the word *curmudgeon* popped into her head; her dad would be proud that she remembered the vocabulary word. He sat with his nose shoved purposefully into a newspaper, shaking his head at something he was reading. A mug that read I'M CRABBY TILL I GET MY COFFEE sat near his right hand, and Fairday hoped he'd already had his cup of joe, if the logo on the mug was accurate. Holding tightly to her folder, she walked up to him and lightly tapped him on the shoulder.

"Hi, um, Mr. Lovell," she said.

Fairday stepped back a bit as he jumped in his seat and blurted, "What?" Turning his head around to see who had touched him, he grumbled, "I'm not a door."

"I'm sorry. Hi, Mr. Lovell, I'm Fairday Morrow," she said, extending a friendly hand.

"Ah! Hello, Miss Morrow." His voice warmed up immediately. "I have been anticipating our meeting today. I'm so glad to meet you." He stood up and shook her hand. "Have a seat, please." Larry Lovell pulled out a chair for her and then moved to the other side of the table. "You startled me. I was involved in a story and wasn't expecting to get poked by someone." He looked at her as he folded the paper and then rested his elbows purposefully on the table.

"Sorry about that," she replied again, hoping she hadn't started things off on the wrong foot. Fairday wasn't feeling very in control of the situation and started to wonder just who was the interviewer and who was the interviewee. He leaned over the table and seemed to study her from behind his wire-rim glasses, which were perched on top of his bumpy old nose.

"Well, uh, so, thanks again for meeting with me," she said, not sure how to begin. Fidgeting with her folder, Fairday pulled out her sheet of questions. The article about Ruby Begonia was underneath it, but she wasn't ready to introduce that just yet.

"It's my pleasure, young lady." Larry's voice was gruff, but there was a certain trustworthiness to his tone. He peered at her with interest. "Now, what would you like to know?"

"Uh, let's see. I have a few questions about your career as a reporter," she said.

"Shoot."

"Mr. Lovell," she began, trying to sound professional, "what was the biggest story you covered?"

Larry's eyes crinkled at the corners as his mouth spread into a wide grin. "Ah, jumping right in, are we?" he sighed. Leaning back in his chair, he folded his arms across his chest while keeping his gaze on Fairday. "What an interesting question. Incidentally, the story that sticks out most in my mind involves your current address, Miss Morrow." His pale eyes flickered mischievously. "How coincidental, wouldn't you say?"

"The Begonia House?" asked Fairday.

"Yes, my dear, the Begonia House," he mused, rubbing the stumpy hairs on his chin.

The words hung in the air as Fairday's thoughts raced wildly. She realized he was waiting for her to say something. As she started to jot down what he had said, she managed to find her voice and asked, "What was the story about?"

"Oh, it was about many things my dear, many things indeed. If I'm being honest, I wrote more than one article about the house and its mysterious occupants." He paused, giving his head a slight shake, then went on. "It's all very complicated. I think the best thing for me to do is start at the beginning." Larry looked down at her, took a sip of his coffee, and then began his tale. Fairday tried to keep up, taking down each word as fast as she could.

"It was in 1936 when Thurston Begonia finally finished that enormous home, nothing but the best for him and his wife. He built the place for her, you know." His eyebrows rose as he looked her over.

Fairday didn't want to break the spell. She wanted to give him plenty of time to divulge some of the secrets about her house. She smiled, giving Larry an encouraging nod, and looked back down at her notepad.

He went on. "Well, you can imagine—a rich, famous explorer sets up camp in a small town, and everybody takes notice. But he doesn't just set up camp. He builds the largest and most intricate house the town has ever seen. Then or now," he added with emphasis. "Folks couldn't help but want to know all the details. It took a long time to build, so everyone's interest was strong. And for years, it gave people something to talk about while they sat on their front porches." He paused, lost in thought for a moment. "It wasn't long after that when tragedy struck." He lowered his voice as he continued. "Thurston's wife, Cora Lynn, passed away in the house giving birth to their daughter, Ruby."

Fairday's hand stopped for a moment as she processed Larry's words. She knew Ruby's mother had died but didn't realize it had happened in her house. For a moment she wasn't sure she was prepared for the rest of the story.

"I hope I haven't spooked you, my dear. That's not my intention," he said.

Fairday gave him a small smile. "I'm okay, Mr. Lovell. So,

what happened after that? Did Thurston and Ruby stay in the house?" she asked.

"Why, yes, they did. For years Ruby and Thurston went about their lives, though with a great deal of sadness hanging over them. Still, her father was wealthy, and Ruby never wanted for anything. Oh, there were happy times, I'm sure. She grew up with every advantage and eventually met a young man she planned to marry." Shaking his head, he said, "'The Missing Bride' was the first article I covered about the Begonia House. Ruby was set to be married at the family home when she suddenly went missing. Unbelievable, really. There were so many people around, setting up for the biggest event Ashpot had ever seen, and not one person knew what happened to the bride-to-be. The police interviewed everyone on the scene, but there were few clues, and unfortunately, Miss Begonia was never seen nor heard from again."

Fairday felt the hairs on her arms stand up. *He wrote the article!* She had the very article that Larry was talking about. Should she show it to him? Fairday decided to whip it out. "Well, Mr. Lovell, it's interesting that you mention the disappearance of Ruby Begonia, because I found this article upstairs in my house, and I was planning to ask you about it." She forced herself to breathe evenly as she passed it across the table.

Nodding, he read the headline, mouthing the words. "Yes, yes. That was a sad day in Ashpot, and an occurrence her father never got over. Thurston kept to himself after she disappeared, never wanting guests. He had roses delivered every month, but the maid answered the door and was instructed to place them in his study. Her account of what she saw reinforced rumors that the family was cursed. Now, what intrigues me is *where* you found this. Upstairs, you said?" He watched her with interest.

"Um, yes," Fairday answered. "My friend found it in a stack of old newspapers while we were exploring a room on the third floor—"

Before she could finish her sentence, he practically shouted, "You've been up on the third floor? What were you doing there? What about the padlock?" He looked terrified as he rattled off each question.

"Uh, yeah. My father unlocked it so we could see what was up there." She decided to leave out the reason for her father unlocking the door. "Why? Do you know something about the third floor?" Fairday asked.

Breathing deeply, Mr. Lowell replied, "Yes, I think I do. You see . . . the last article I wrote about the house concerned the death of Thurston Begonia. The events of the incident were unclear, but he was found dead outside the home. It was believed he jumped or was pushed off the third-floor balcony—again, a mystery that was never solved. I put the lock on myself and gave the key to the police. I should have known someone would eventually go up there if the house ever sold. Though, honestly, I never believed anyone would think of buying it." His blue eyes drifted to the side and he gazed out the window.

Fairday's heart skipped a beat as a flash of the willow tree coming to life ran through her mind's eye. In almost a whisper, she reiterated, "He fell from the balcony and died?"

"No, my dear. I said it wasn't determined *how* he died. Falling implies it was an accident, and I do *not* believe his death was accidental." He closed his eyes. Clearing his throat, he refocused on Fairday. "Is there anything else you would like to know, Miss Morrow?"

His manner suggested that the interview was coming to an end. Suddenly, Fairday felt panicked. She hadn't asked him anything she could use for the biography project. She began to sift through her papers. Larry seemed to sense her agitation and grabbed her arm. Fairday stopped and looked up at him.

"I was well aware we weren't going to be talking about me this morning, so I took the liberty of writing down some facts about myself for your school project. This should be sufficient," he said, sliding a piece of paper across the table.

Fairday picked it up, a wave of relief washing over her. It seemed he had outlined his entire life. Feeling grateful for this man's clever kindness, she concluded that his grumpy exterior was just a mask. Larry Lovell was definitely an ally. "Thank you so much. I really appreciate all of this," she said, standing up and pushing her chair back.

She walked over to him and extended her hand. Grasping it tightly, he pulled her in closer. In a hushed tone, he said, "Be careful, Miss Morrow. That house is not to be taken lightly." He squeezed her hand harder as he continued. "As I said, there are people who believe the family had some kind of evil curse placed on them and that there's something not quite right about the home." He released his grip and settled back into his chair.

Fairday stood there staring at Larry Lovell. He had just confirmed that whatever it was she and Lizzy were dealing with was real, and it was definitely dangerous. "Um, thanks again, Mr. Lovell, for everything. I won't take it lightly." She didn't know what to say. Should she tell him about the things she had found? Should she tell him about the sneaker? What about the lady in the mirror and the tree that had tried to grab her? *Holy cow!* Fairday thought in bewilderment. Could that have been how Thurston Begonia had died? Was he pulled off the balcony?

These questions must have been written across her forehead, because no sooner had she thought them than Larry said, "Remember, young lady, you have to think beyond what you know to be real. You have to see with your mind as well as your eyes." He pulled his glasses down to the end of his nose and looked at her. "And if you ever need my help, just call, and I'll be there." He then turned back to his newspaper, which he shook lightly in the air, and began reading.

Fairday spotted Lizzy sitting at a table with her face inches away from a computer. She was clicking the mouse as she moved it back and forth. Leaning over her shoulder, pointing to something on the screen, was none other than Brocket the Rocket. *This should be interesting,* thought Fairday, and she hurried across the library to meet her friends.

# ∾ NINETEEN ∾

## THE RIGHT ANSWER

Fairday stepped up behind Marcus and Lizzy. "Hi, guys," she said, poking both of them on the shoulder. They looked up at her in surprise. "I see you two have met." Fairday smirked, trying to give her best friend the eye signal that this was *the* Brocket the Rocket she had told her about. Lizzy gave a quick nod, acknowledging that she had already put that together.

"Yeah, I was busy working on enhancing the image when I was interrupted by advice being thrown at me," Lizzy said, pointing a thumb in Marcus's direction as she rolled her eyes, but there was warmth in her voice.

"What?" Marcus replied. "Don't tell me my advice wasn't helpful. You did what I said, and it worked!" He nodded confidently. Lizzy's laughter rang out, catching the sharp ears of the librarian. She glared at them and put a finger to her lips.

Fairday gave her an apologetic grin, then turned back to the screen. Leaning between her friends, she whispered, "So what've you got?"

"Well, it took a while, but I enhanced the writing on the back of the picture, and I was able to decipher what it says. Look at this—you're going to freak out." Lizzy pointed to the monitor, which displayed the blurry but legible writing from the back. "So Ruby Begonia knew about the key."

Before Fairday could respond, Marcus blurted out, "Who's Ruby Begonia?" The two girls quickly focused their eyes on Marcus, who immediately took a step back. "I don't want to butt in or anything, but this sounds really interesting."

Both girls smiled as they shot each other an approving glance. "Okay, Marcus, you want in?" Lizzy asked.

"In on what?" Marcus replied.

"In on the DMS," said Fairday, pausing for effect before spelling it out. "The Detective Mystery Squad."

Lizzy chimed in. "It's our club. We piece together evidence to uncover the truth about unsolved cases. I'm the head technical supervisor, and Fairday's the senior investigator." She nodded importantly at Fairday. "We've been in business for two years."

"Really?" Marcus eyed them suspiciously. "What've you solved so far?"

"That's classified," Fairday said. "Only members of the DMS have access to that information, though a bunch of people have tried to join."

"Well, what would I have to do to join? If I wanted to, that is." Marcus seemed a little nervous.

Lizzy kept her eyes glued to his as she said in her most serious tone, "You have to answer a question."

"That's it?" he said.

"That's it," Lizzy replied, then added, "I mean, no one has ever answered it correctly, but you seem pretty smart . . . maybe you'll get it."

Marcus's eyes lit up. "One question? I think I can handle that." His confidence was leaking out his ears. Fairday couldn't help but laugh as he exclaimed, "No problem!"

"All right, then," Lizzy said as she stood up from her chair. "I vote we initiate Brocket the Rocket into the DMS. Fairday, what do you think?" Marcus looked stunned that Lizzy knew his nickname, but before he could open his mouth to speak, she put her hand on his shoulder. "Yes, yes, I know all sorts of stuff about you, Marcus Brocket," she said in her most studious voice. "Your dad is in the FBI and your nickname is Brocket the Rocket because you run really fast. The DMS is known for having all the facts straight before initiating anyone into its society."

Marcus stood there with his mouth open. Fairday could tell Lizzy had impressed him. Her ease with people always took them by surprise. Fairday bent in close to Lizzy and whispered, "He's cool. We should let him in—if he gets the riddle, that is." Both girls turned to face Marcus, whose nerves seemed to be wavering once again.

The question they had decided to use for initiation into the DMS was a version of an ancient riddle, but Fairday thought it was perfect. She and Lizzy had spent days poring over books and joke magazines to come up with a really hard question that only the extraordinarily quick-witted could answer. Lizzy had found it in one of Fairday's favorite books, *Dragons and Other Fabulous Beasts*. The solution to the riddle was simple enough, though even Fairday wondered if she would've guessed it correctly without the book. But that didn't matter. The club belonged to her and Lizzy, and they both knew how clever they were.

"Okay, Marcus. What goes on four legs, on two, and at last on three?" asked Fairday.

A smile spread across his face, and he seemed to regain his self-assured composure. "Hmm, what goes on four legs, two legs, and at last on three? Let's see. . . ." He paused, scratching his chin for effect.

Lizzy shoved him in the arm as she exclaimed, "Just say it if you know it!"

"I think the answer is . . . ," Marcus said, drawing it out.

Lizzy nudged him again when he continued to scratch his chin. Finally, he blurted out, "Man!"

"Nicely done! How'd you know the answer?" Fairday asked.

"It's the Riddle of the Sphinx. Mythology's kind of my thing," Marcus bragged.

The librarian looked up sternly, and Fairday said, "Let's get out of here."

"You betcha!" Lizzy replied. "Congratulations, Brocket the Rocket. You're in." She emphasized his nickname as she beamed at him.

Lizzy scribbled down the writing from the picture onto a notepad, then stuffed it into her DMS pack. She logged off of the computer, and they made their way across the room, feeling the librarian's eyes following them all the way out.

The DMS descended the steps of the library, Marcus listening as Lizzy filled him in about the Detective Mystery Squad and the case they were investigating. "So, I mean, the things we found in the house all point to Ruby Begonia being the—" Before Lizzy could finish, she was interrupted by someone yelling.

"Hey, Bart, look, it's Brocket the Dork and Freakday. What are they, like, married now or something? And who's the fat girl?" Dif's words were directed at Marcus, Lizzy, and Fairday, rather than Bart. He was dressed in black, wearing his army jacket, his buzzed hair coated in oily gel. Bart and Sadie flocked around him.

Bart joined in Dif's taunting and began to chant, "Freakday and Brocket sittin' in a tree . . ." Sadie, on the other hand, looked uncomfortable. She had a shy expression on her face and was blushing as she moved away from the boys.

Marcus walked down the steps and right up to Dif. They were eye to eye as he said, "Hey, Dif, taking your pets for a walk?"

"I oughta kick your butt right now, Brocket. You need to step off," Dif spat out.

Suddenly, Lizzy pushed past Fairday, flipped her curls, and walked right into the middle of the confrontation. She addressed Sadie cheerfully, extending her hand in welcome. "Hi, I'm Lizzy. What's your name?"

Sadie seemed confused, as did the boys, whose anger began to dissipate. She stared at Lizzy for several moments, then shook her hand and smiled.

"Hi, I'm Sadie. It's really nice to meet you. Are you one of Fairday's friends from New York City?" she asked, moving even farther away from Dif.

All eyes were on the girls as Dif backed away from Marcus. Lizzy answered, "Yes, I am. It's nice to meet you too! I hope we get a chance to hang out sometime." She calmly turned her attention on Dif. "Dif, is it? I wouldn't go around making fun of people if I were you. It doesn't win you any friends."

Dif was speechless. Lizzy had managed, yet again, to make another boy's mouth drop open. Marcus seemed impressed by her boldness and how unaffected she was by Dif calling her fat. Fairday and Lizzy shared the belief that, as long as you are true to yourself, and happy with who you are, no one can hurt you with their words.

The DMS walked away from Dif and his gang and Fairday noticed Sadie was now by herself, crossing to the other side of the street. She was heading for the ice cream shop where girls from their class were gathered out front, laughing and eating whipped cream sundaes.

# TWENTY

## TRAPPED INSIDE!

It was decided that the DMS would meet after lunch to work on the case. Marcus lived right over the hill from Fairday. He told them there was a trail that started in his yard and went through the woods that led up to the Begonia House. Fairday and Lizzy promised to be at the front gate around three o'clock. He turned back and waved to them, mouthing, "See you later," as he climbed into his father's pickup truck.

"I can't believe how cool Marcus is!" Lizzy said.

"Yeah. I'm glad he's in the DMS," Fairday replied.

"Girls! I'm here!" Mrs. Morrow called out. She looked frazzled as she pulled up to them.

"Hi, Mom," Fairday said as she climbed into the car. "How'd it go?"

"Ugh, it was a pain, as I knew it would be. I was happy to get your text so I could get out of that place. Anyway, we have to pick up Margo from day care, and then we can finally go home. Hallelujah! I hope she had a good day, or we're all in for it."

Fairday and Lizzy walked down to the front gate after they had eaten a fast lunch of ham and cheese sandwiches, accompanied by what was known in the Morrow family as "Mouse Fillets," which were skinned pickles thinly sliced into mini-fillets—another one of Mr. Morrow's creative food endeavors. Fairday had to give him credit; they were delicious and much more interesting than having a plain pickle. She opened up the front gate, and the two girls waited for Marcus to arrive.

"So, what do you think about the writing on the picture?" Lizzy asked, looking down at the note she had scribbled. "'Father, I'm here!'" she read aloud. "'Beware the tree when you use the key, turn around and you will see . . .'"

"I wish there was more. I wonder why she stopped writing," Fairday said. "And if it was in the frame, how would her father have seen it? And where is she? In the mirror?"

"I don't know, but I'll tell you one thing. I don't think whatever we saw in the mirror is human. I mean, she was really creepy-looking, and her hair seemed alive or something!" Lizzy said.

"I agree. I don't think that was Ruby Begonia either. She looked like the lady in the picture, except the woman in the mirror seemed evil or possessed. Do you think someone could be disguising themselves as her?" Fairday asked.

Before Lizzy could add her thoughts on the subject, the rumbling sounds of a revving engine speeding up the road tore through the air.

"What's that?" Lizzy shouted. Her question was answered almost immediately. Brocket the Rocket was racing up the hill, riding a red ATV. He slowed as he reached the gate.

"Hey," Marcus said coolly, taking off his helmet. Pointing at his black backpack, he added, "I brought some stuff with me."

"Marcus Brocket, I must say, I had no idea you were going to arrive in such style!" Lizzy said as she walked over and ran her fingers over the handlebars.

He chuckled. "I guess I'm just full of surprises." He smiled at Lizzy, who looked away, blushing. Fairday laughed to herself at her best friend's obvious interest in the new member of the DMS.

Up in the third-floor room, the three detectives sat in a circle with all of the evidence they had gathered spread out in front of them. Auntie Em was sniffing around, searching for a comfortable spot to snooze. Fairday and Lizzy had just finished going over everything with Marcus, taking turns to produce the clues in the same order that Fairday had shown Lizzy. They enjoyed watching Marcus's facial expressions as each piece was presented. His face was a mixture of awe and determination. Although they used the ultraviolet light and the infrared goggles that Marcus had "borrowed" from his dad, nothing new was revealed.

Finally, they put the evidence aside and examined the picture Lizzy had enhanced. Fairday took out the notebook and pen and set them down next to her. "Okay, here we go," she said as she began reading the clue from the back of the picture. "This is the first line: 'Father, I'm here!'" She paused for a moment to let the words sink in, and then added, "So that must mean that Ruby was still in the house and hadn't gone anywhere, right?" She bit the end of her pen.

"Yeah, that makes sense," Marcus responded. "But why? Did she write this after she went missing?"

Lizzy chimed in, "You betcha! She must have, because it was the picture taken on her wedding day. Ruby wouldn't have seen it before she disappeared. That's why she was trying to tell him she hadn't died or gone missing."

Fairday continued. "'Beware the tree when you use the key.' The key mentioned here must be the one that opens the balcony door, because we know she's definitely talking about the willow. I mean, we saw it come alive, and it tried to make a grab for me!" She pointed to her ankle. "Mr. Lovell said Ruby's dad, Thurston, died when he fell from the third-floor balcony. He implied that he didn't think it was accidental, and I'm pretty sure, after reading this"—she held up the picture and shook it—"and actually seeing it for myself, that he was pulled over by that tree!" There was a moment of silence as they looked at each other in amazement. Fairday went on, breaking the spell. "It says here, too, 'Turn around and you will see.' When we turned around after the tree tried to attack us, we saw the evil-looking red-haired lady staring at us from inside the mirror."

"And," Lizzy piped up, "we think the mirror's the way in." She pointed in its direction. "After all, Margo almost went all the way through a door that appeared in it. That's when she pulled out this sneaker." Lizzy grabbed the sparkling red shoe and held it up.

"The way into where, though?" Marcus asked as he took the sneaker from Lizzy and turned it over in his hands. His eyes widened as he held it, clearly feeling the odd vibrations. He passed it back to Lizzy with a look of uncertainty on his face.

She took the sneaker from him and began to shove it back into her DMS pack with the rest of the clues. "What's really crazy is the fact that this sneaker fits me perfectly!"

"Yeah," Fairday said. "I mean, what are the chances of finding a magical shoe that actually fits? It's like something out of *The Wizard of Oz*."

"I wonder what would happen if you wore both shoes," Marcus said.

"I don't know, but in the book Dorothy doesn't realize the shoes have powers, only the witch does. When each of them has a shoe, the magic is divided. The trick is you have to know how to make them work. Imagine if these are like those!" Fairday said, grabbing her best friend's arm.

"Oh my gosh! That would be so cool!" Lizzy gushed, grinning with excitement.

"Okay, let's focus," Marcus interrupted. "Where do you guys think the mirror goes?"

"I have no idea," Fairday answered. "I mean, where could it possibly go?" She threw her hands in the air.

"Anything's possible," Lizzy said.

"Yeah, that's for sure. Larry Lovell did mention something about Thurston Begonia that I wanted to tell you. Hang on, I have the interview right here," Fairday said, rummaging through her pack for her school folder. Whipping out the paper, she scanned her notes until she came to the part about Thurston. "Mr. Lovell told me Thurston Begonia kept to himself, never wanting guests. But every month after Ruby went missing, he had roses delivered. Supposedly the maid was instructed to place them in

Thurston's study. Rumors about the family being cursed were reinforced by the gossip she spread about the wild things she saw in there."

"Do you have any idea which room was his study?" Lizzy asked.

"Well, there's a room on the second floor with a desk in it, and there's other stuff in there too! It's all covered up with sheets, but it could've been his study. I discovered it the first day we moved in, when I was picking out my bedroom."

"We should check it out," Marcus said. "Who knows what we'll find."

"I think we should definitely take a look," Fairday replied. "What do you think, Lizzy?"

"You betcha!" Lizzy exclaimed, clapping her hands. "Let's get going!"

Auntie Em seemed to understand something was happening and lifted an eyelid at Lizzy's raised voice. She sat up, eyes bugged out, panting in Fairday's direction.

"Is Auntie Em okay up here by herself or should we bring her with us?" Lizzy asked.

"She's fine. Besides, we'll be back soon," Fairday said, bending down to pat her dog's head. "You stay here, all right, girl?" Auntie Em wagged her knobby tail twice before she plopped back down, her puggish snore starting up again.

# TWENTY-ONE

## SECRETS ON THE SHELVES

Creaking open the door, the three detectives slipped into the room. The green velvet curtains were drawn, making the space feel dark and dank. Everything was dusty, including the massive wooden desk, which sat in front of the window. Marcus walked over to it and pulled back the adjacent curtains to let some light in. He then began opening the drawers. Lizzy started pulling sheets off, revealing a brown leather armchair and a large globe set in an iron frame.

Fairday walked over to the other side of the room and pulled off a sheet. To her surprise, the first thing she uncovered was an antique bookcase. Most of the books were in relatively good shape, while the bindings of others were coming undone. There were many leather-bound editions with ornate covers, and she breathed in the old books, relishing their musty smell. Leaning in, she read the titles on the closest shelf: *Master Manifestations: How to Make Your Dreams Come True* by Dorian Stark. *Mix Your Own Mayhem* by I. L. Notso. *Magic Forthcoming* by Edith Goodsoe. What an amazing find! Fairday couldn't wait to curl up on the chair in here and do some reading. She'd always been fascinated by magic, and these books sounded like hours of entertainment.

"Guys, check this out! I might have something that can point us in the right direction."

Lizzy and Marcus both stopped what they were doing and hurried to her side. Fairday pointed to *Remembering Ruby* by T. S. Begonia. "I don't believe it—Thurston must've written a book about Ruby!" Fairday pulled it down, blew the dust off, and flipped open the cover.

"Oh my gosh! I never would've expected that!" Lizzy exclaimed as Fairday held it out for her partners to see. It wasn't a book at all. Instead of pages, the interior was hollowed out like a box and packed with dried rose petals.

"Why would Thurston have done this?" Fairday asked, remembering the rose petals she had found on the floor of the third-floor room and the one in Ruby's diary. *What do they mean?*

"Dump them out," Marcus interjected. "Maybe there's a clue stuffed in there."

Lizzy rolled her eyes at Marcus's crude words but nodded

in agreement. Fairday began to walk over to the desk when suddenly a strong breeze blew in, slamming the door shut. They all jumped. The petals flew out of the box from the sudden gust of wind, fluttering down softly as the room became still once again.

"Where did the wind come from?" Fairday asked with a shiver. "The windows aren't even open."

"Creepy," Lizzy answered.

"This is definitely not the Saturday I was expecting when I went to the library today," Marcus said. "This is awesome! I'd like to think it could be a ghost, but chances are there's air coming in from cracks around the window, which created a draft."

"I hope so," Fairday said, gnawing on her thumbnail. The anxiety she felt from the last ghostly appearance flooded through her body. *No more sightings, thank goodness,* she thought.

Examining the empty book, they were disappointed there was nothing behind the space where the petals had been resting.

"That doesn't make sense," Marcus said. "Why would Thurston create this fake book only to hide dead roses in it? There must be more to it." Bending down, he grabbed his black light from his pack and closed the curtains as the purple light began to fill the room. As he waved it over the book, a sliver of white showed in the hollowed out area. "There's something here, but I can't find a way to it."

"Pull off the cover and see if there's anything on the other side of the space," Fairday directed.

Marcus eased it off. Running his hands over it under the glowing light, he saw a dark spot. "A hinge!" he exclaimed. Whipping open the curtains, he turned off his black light.

Fairday kept her eyes on the book as Marcus slid the hidden hinge aside, revealing another secret compartment. Only this one wasn't filled with rose petals. Nor was it empty.

# TWENTY-TWO

## TAKEN BY SURPRISE

Snatching up the note, Fairday scanned it and exclaimed, "Oh my goodness! Listen to this! 'Dear Ruby, I know you're here. Sometimes I think I catch a glimpse of you turning a corner. I can't see you, though I feel you in the air around me. I know you can read my words, even though there aren't any that can express my sorrow. Roses were always your favorite flower, and you will always be . . .' Ugh, the note is ripped in half. It ends there. What a peculiar place to hide a letter."

"It sure is! But that note definitely makes a case for the house being haunted," Marcus said.

"Oh, that doesn't make me feel any better. Do you think that was what rushed past us and slammed the door before? A ghost?" Fairday paled at the thought.

"I don't know, but we *do* know that Thurston didn't think he was alone after Ruby disappeared. It might also help to explain the writing on the back of the picture. We just need to figure out where she went and what happened to her."

"Larry Lovell told me to go beyond what could be seen with my eyes," Fairday said.

Just then, a screeching note sounded in the hallway, causing them to jump.

"What was that?" Marcus yelled.

Dread seeped over Fairday like molasses. "Bagpipes," she said, sounding scared.

Auntie Em barked. They could hear her continue to howl and then whimper from the third floor. Lizzy's mouth dropped open as Fairday shot out of the room and began racing to the third floor. Marcus and Lizzy were right behind her when they reached the top step and saw the little pug being carried over the shoulder of the red-haired lady through the door in the mirror.

"Auntie Em!" Fairday cried, rushing toward the scene. She touched the mirror, but it was solid. "Oh my goodness! What should we do? She's got Auntie Em! We have to save her!"

"Don't worry, Fairday. We'll get her back!" Lizzy said.

"We don't know that!" Fairday sobbed.

Marcus put on a brave face and said with conviction, "Let's open up that old mirror and get your dog back. Whoever is haunting this house needs to be stopped. Since the

clue on the picture says to use the key and turn around, maybe that's how to get inside the mirror."

Fairday nodded weakly as Lizzy said, "That sounds like a plan. We just have to remember to keep an eye on that tree."

The DMS stood in front of the mirror, seeing only their reflections looking back at them. "Okay," Fairday said. "Here's the brass key." She held it up, feeling somewhat like her father with his key announcements. "We need to open the balcony door." She once again pulled back the caution tape and thrust the key into the lock, turning it. Marcus and Lizzy stood behind her; she could feel their breath on the back of her neck as the door swung open, revealing the balcony.

"Whoa!" Marcus exclaimed as he leaned over Fairday's shoulder to get a better look. "I can see your dad's reasoning behind putting up all the caution tape. It definitely doesn't look safe!"

"Just wait," Lizzy said, holding on to the strap of Fairday's DMS pack and bracing herself in the doorjamb.

The wind began to pick up and Fairday poked Marcus in the side, pointing to the willow tree. The bluish leaves began to come alive on the twisted limbs, which were contorting and extending up toward the balcony, growing at an alarming rate. The wind howled furiously as the tree bent toward them, reaching up with its long, twisted fingers.

"Holy cow!" Marcus shouted. "It's gonna grab us!"

"Everyone turn around!" Lizzy yelled above the sound of the rushing wind and colliding branches. Quickly turning, they faced the mirror. The door was there, and it was open, but there was no sign of the terrifying lady.

The space they were standing in was now glowing with a bluish hue. Branches were pushing their way in through the door. One limb wrapped itself around Marcus's waist and was beginning to drag him out onto the balcony. "STOP, STOP!" he bellowed, panicking as he tried to yank it off.

Fairday went to grab Marcus but was forcefully flung

backward and propelled through the mirror. She let out a yelp of surprise as she landed on her butt, wincing from the pain that shot up her back. Shaking her head to try to get a semblance of where she was and what was going on, she gave a cry of shock as she looked around. Was she the only member of the DMS who had made it through the mirror? Her mouth dropped open in awe as she speculated on what she had just done and how she would ever get back.

# TWENTY-THREE

## THE OTHER BEGONIA HOUSE

Pulling herself up, Fairday felt like she had been transported into some sort of strange dream. She was alone and standing before the mirror, which no longer reflected a doorway but appeared more like a window. On the other side, the balcony door was closed; there was no sign of the raging willow, only remnants of ripped caution tape. She reached out and gently touched the mirror. It was solid and smooth beneath her fingertips. Fairday pressed her whole palm against the mirror and tried to calm down, but her thoughts galloped wildly in circles around her head. *Are we stuck here?*

Focusing on the present once more, she noticed how quiet it had become. Without the chaos from only moments ago, her surroundings now seemed too still. Suddenly, she heard what sounded like a creaking step. Remembering the archway, she spun around to face it. The sound grew louder, and Fairday backed herself up against the wall. Who or what was heading her way?

She relaxed when she recognized the familiar blond curls ascending the staircase. Lizzy emerged, followed by Marcus, both of them looking quite disheveled; Lizzy's hair was a tangled mess of sticks and dead leaves, while Marcus's shirt was covered with dirt and what looked like blood. A gash in his cheek was bleeding, and his legs had long scratches. Fairday looked down at herself, but other than a few scrapes, she seemed to be all right.

"What happened?" she asked.

"Well, once I saw the branches rushing toward us, and you fly backwards, I grabbed Marcus and jumped into the mirror, pulling as hard as I could," Lizzy explained.

"Yeah, you pulled hard," Marcus said. "I only had time to slam the balcony door closed before we rolled halfway down the spiral staircase. Fairday's lucky she didn't have to take that trip."

"It definitely doesn't look like it was fun," Fairday replied. Thankfully, though, they were all in one piece, and other than Marcus's cut, which seemed to have stopped bleeding, no one had suffered anything more serious. After brushing themselves off, the three then focused on their situation.

They were standing in the middle of the third-floor landing. To their right was the secret room, to the left was the balcony, and in front of them stood the mirror. As similar as everything looked, it was all completely different. Their surroundings appeared to be newer and much cleaner. The floorboards were gleaming and both of the wall sconces were lit, whereas on the other side only one of them had a working bulb, while the other was broken and falling off its hook. There were no cobwebs or spiders. It all seemed newly decorated; all of it, that is, except the mirror, which looked as ancient as it ever had.

"Where are we? And how are we going to get out of here?" Marcus asked.

"I already touched the mirror. It looks more like a window now. I couldn't see a door or any other reflection." Fairday shrugged. "I don't know how, but we're in my house, only it's not my house."

"Weird," Lizzy mumbled as she walked over to the balcony door and peered outside. Excitedly, she yelled, "You guys have got to see this!"

Fairday and Marcus looked down at the balcony before stepping onto it. It seemed sturdy, no longer creaking and dilapidated. Walking out a bit farther, they looked down at the backyard and in unison exclaimed, "Wow!" Except this time it had nothing to do with the wild willow tree.

"Are they ghosts?" Marcus asked.

"They look like what I picture ghosts to look like," Lizzy murmured.

The three detectives stood transfixed by what they were witnessing. The deadened area that Fairday knew to be her backyard was bursting with life, or possibly just the memory of life. It was green and drenched in sunlight, accented by colorful flowers, which cascaded through multiple gardens and stone pathways. An arbor dripping with leafy vines was set up under the willow, which was blooming peacefully. Its branches swayed in a soft breeze, and Fairday flinched as she watched them move, bracing herself in case they decided to suddenly come to life and reach out for her. But the oddest thing about the backyard was the hazy figures of people dressed in fancy clothes, walking around and talking among themselves. They were just dim shadows, dancing and cavorting with each other against a background of color and life.

"Hey!" Lizzy shouted. "Hey down there!" But no one looked up. The ghostly figures just walked about, chatting and smiling. "Strange. Let's see if the three of us can get their attention. Maybe they can't hear me from this far up."

The DMS tried with all their might to get a reaction from the ghost people. But no one gave any indication they heard them.

"Hold on a sec. Let me try my night-vision goggles," Marcus said, taking them out of his backpack and putting them on. "Holy cow! They're gone! Those figures have no heat, so they can't be real people."

"Let me try!" Lizzy exclaimed, and Marcus handed them to her.

"The infrared light senses temperature, and the hotter the object, the brighter it looks. It's dark where those figures are. Humans would glow," he explained.

"I see what you mean," Lizzy said, passing the goggles to Fairday.

"Eerie as it is, at least those ghosts don't seem scary," Fairday said, handing the goggles back to Marcus, who put them in his bag.

"All right, that's enough," said Lizzy. Fumbling with her DMS pack and pulling it onto her shoulders, she added, "We need to find Auntie Em and figure out what the heck is going on here!"

Fairday and Marcus adjusted their own packs, then stood next to Lizzy, ready to begin investigating the other Begonia House.

# ~TWENTY-FOUR~

## FEAR NOT THE UNEXPECTED

The DMS was united but weary. They entered the third-floor room, a mixture of fear and excitement creeping in with them.

"Would you look at that," Lizzy whispered. "It's set up like someone's actually using it as a bedroom." She walked over to the chair, which was still in the corner, and trailed her fingers over the smooth, striped fabric.

There were no boxes piled up on the floor or dust bunnies wafting through the room or spiders scuttling about. Instead, it seemed to sparkle in the afternoon sunlight. The wardrobe was still there, its iron claws clamped together. There was also a four-poster bed, which was made up with a red velvet coverlet and silk pillows. Across from the bed was a wooden vanity with three candles lit on top. Fancy perfume bottles were arranged in rows, and in the center was a shining silver hand mirror, which shimmered under the candles' glow.

"Fairday, hand me the brush!" Lizzy shouted. Fairday jumped in fright at the sudden outburst but quickly followed her instructions. Momentarily fumbling through her DMS pack, she whipped out the hairbrush and thrust it into her friend's outstretched hand.

"Well, look at that," Lizzy mumbled, more to herself than to her companions. "It's so shiny and new. And look! There's a place for it here!" She pointed to a spot next to the mirror. "It's a set."

"So," Marcus said, "it seems that on this side of the mirror, things are as they once were, like they're stuck in time or something."

"Yeah," replied Fairday. "Except the mirror we just came through still looks exactly the same."

Lizzy placed the brush next to the hand mirror and turned to face Marcus and Fairday. "How do you think all this is possible? Clearly someone's been in here. I mean, who lit these candles?"

"I think we have to assume that anything is possible from here on out, and that we are definitely not alone," Marcus said.

"He's right," Lizzy responded first. "All we have to go on is what we know so far. Let's hope it's enough to get us out of here alive."

Fairday couldn't help but recoil at Lizzy's words. *Get out of here alive?* It seemed so dramatic—ridiculous, really. But hadn't Larry Lovell told her more than one person had died in this house? The tree *had* come to life and tried to grab them, hadn't it? Was it really possible that their very lives were in danger? Yes was the answer her mind instantly shot back; their lives were in danger, and they needed to find her dog and a way out before the red-haired woman, whoever she was, figured out they were traipsing through her place.

"Well, let's have a look around, then, and try to find Auntie Em," Marcus said. "Quietly, though. I don't think whoever lives here knows we've arrived."

"Which is strange," Lizzy replied. "We made such a racket when we came through the mirror, I would've thought we alerted just about every living thing within fifty miles of us."

Marcus raised his eyebrows. "*Living* being the key word—maybe that's your answer. Those ghosts didn't seem to hear us when we were screaming our heads off at them."

"But," Fairday interjected, "the red-haired lady doesn't look like a shadow or a ghost. She's as real-looking as anything."

"Yeah, that's for sure," Lizzy said. "Okay, time's ticking. We better get moving!"

Three backpacks were flung onto the bed, and the DMS went to work. Marcus pulled out his infrared goggles again and strapped them to his head. Spinning around, he pointed his finger at Lizzy and Fairday. "Never fear, Brocket's here!" he whispered dramatically, pushing his chin up, and the girls couldn't hold back their laughter.

"I know they're cool and all, but you really do look ridiculous," Lizzy said through her snickers as she continued to fasten the headlamp around her curls.

"Just like a superhero detective! Watch out, world, here comes Brocket the Rocket!" Fairday chuckled.

"Ha-ha," Marcus said. "Just you wait." He smiled. "You're gonna be even more thankful you brought me along."

"We'll see." Lizzy nudged him jokingly. "Let's get to work, then, Mr. Superhero Detective."

Fairday began checking the rest of the clues in her backpack to see if anything else looked different on this side. She placed the sneaker and the frame on the bed. Grabbing the hourglass, she noticed that the red sand had turned green. "Check this out!" she said, holding it up. "How could it have changed color?"

"Wow! Weird! It's still stopped, though," Lizzy replied.

"Maybe it has something to do with being on this side of the mirror," Marcus said.

"That makes sense," Fairday said as she continued to fumble around the bottom of her DMS pack. "Oh no! The key! It's not in here; we must have left it on the other side. Unless . . . did you grab it, Lizzy?"

Lizzy reached into her pockets. "No, I don't have it. It must still be in the lock to the balcony door," she said regretfully.

"Oh well," Fairday replied, shrugging. "Who knows if it would've even worked on this side. We'll just have to find another way out." Once again reaching into her DMS pack, she produced the bag containing the red hair they had found in the bristles of the brush. Yelping loudly, she dropped it on the floor.

"What is it?" Lizzy asked, racing over to her side.

"Look!" Fairday pointed at the bag. The hair was glowing red, slithering back and forth inside.

"Ugh! That's so gross!" Lizzy said.

"Yeah, it is gross, but it's also cool," Marcus said as he picked up the bag. Holding it at eye level, he continued to scrutinize the hair. "I just don't understand how it's moving! Any ideas?"

Fairday pulled out a small water bottle from her pack and began to unscrew the top.

"What are you doing?" Marcus asked.

"Well, you might think it's silly, but I know Dorothy was able to melt the wicked witch with water, and I figured it couldn't hurt to bring it along. I'll keep it handy in case the hair gets loose. You never know!" Fairday said.

"I love how you're always prepared!" Lizzy beamed at her partner.

"Okay, what's the plan?" Marcus asked.

"Let's start on the first floor and work our way back up," Fairday suggested.

"Agreed," Lizzy and Marcus answered in unison.

Shoving everything into their packs, they prepared to leave. "Wait," Lizzy all but shouted. "We have to document this. We don't know what's important, and a picture or two could be the answer we need." She opened her pack, took out her camera, and snapped several shots of their surroundings. Lizzy then zoomed in on the matching mirror and even pulled the bag with the hair back out and shot a short video clip. When everything that seemed relevant was documented, Lizzy slipped the camera into the front pocket of her jeans for easy access, and the team was finally ready.

They made their way single file down the spiral staircase. When they came to the door at the bottom of the stairs, their backs stiffened with anticipation as they prepared to turn the corner and explore the rest of the strange world they had tumbled into.

Fairday reached out and turned the knob; the door swung open. Creeping into the second-floor hallway, they peered down the narrow corridor to find the same wall sconces as in Fairday's home illuminating the paintings lining the walls. They were still gaudy; however, all were hanging properly and lacked the thick layer of dust they had accumulated on the other side. Fairday recalled feeling like the faces had been watching her on several occasions.

Goose bumps popped up on her arms as she approached the nearest one: a robust woman with three bobbing chins held back by a string of pearls, which looked like they were going to pop at any second. She had a haughty look on her face, and her nose was turned up in disgust, as if there were a nasty smell. The portrait looked just as unpleasant on this side of the house.

"Now, that's the scariest thing I've seen yet," Marcus said.

"They seem like regular paintings on this side, so lifeless. I remember feeling like they were watching me when I first saw them. It was really bizarre." Hesitantly, Fairday reached out and touched the face of the lady.

"Oh my gosh!" Lizzy exclaimed, and Fairday turned to see what she was talking about. Lizzy was staring at another portrait a few feet down the hall.

"What is it?" Fairday hurried to her partner's side.

"Look into her eyes," Lizzy instructed, her voice wavering. The painting was of a dainty young woman with cascading brown hair.

"Do you know who this is?" Fairday asked.

"Who is . . ." But before Lizzy could get the question out, realization dawned on her. "You're right!" she said.

"Who?" Marcus asked, trying to catch up as he glanced back and forth at both girls.

"It's the lady from the picture I found online. The one with Thurston Begonia unveiling the Begonia House," Lizzy said.

"Oh, right," Marcus said. "This is the woman who was standing next to him. His wife maybe?"

"Cora Lynn Begonia," Fairday said. "Larry Lovell told me she died giving birth to Ruby in this house. I'm sure that's her. I mean, it's got to be, right?"

"Creepy," Lizzy mumbled. "Now check out the eyes." She pointed to the painting.

Fairday moved in and peered into the painting's eyes. "That's my mom! And Margo!" She was breathing fast as she belted out, "Mom! Mom! I'm here! Can you hear me?" Fairday banged on the wall, trying to get her mother's attention.

Through the eyes of the painting, she could clearly see her mother in the hallway bending down to pick up Margo, who was fussing with Mr. Fazzy, her stuffed pony. "Honey, we have to get you changed. Come on now, leave Mr. Fazzy there. You can get him after we get you a clean diapy," Mrs. Morrow said.

"Margo!" Fairday yelled again. "It's me! Look over here!"

"They can't hear you," Marcus said.

"Wait!" Lizzy said. "Look!" Margo had stopped trying to reach for her toy and was looking in the direction of Fairday's voice. "I think she heard you."

"Margo! I'm here!" Fairday shouted once more, her heart racing.

Margo pointed a pudgy finger at the painting and gurgled, "Far-fey!"

"Where's Fairday, snookykins? You want to see your sister? What a love bug you are." Mrs. Morrow kissed her face and carried her down the hallway.

Margo continued to point at the painting. "Far-fey, Far-fey!" she exclaimed in her deceptively wise baby voice.

The last thing Fairday heard was Mrs. Morrow chirping happily, "We'll see Fairday later, sweetie; she's playing with her friends. Here we are, the clean-bottom caboose!" And they disappeared behind one of the doors.

Fairday's chest heaved as she leaned against the wall for support. She began to worry she'd never be with her family again. "What if we can't find Auntie Em and get out of here?" she said, unable to hold back her sobs. "What are we going to do?"

Lizzy placed a hand on her shoulder and helped her to stand up straight. "We're going to be fine," she said. "We'll find her and a way out, I promise."

"It's going to be all right," Marcus said with a warm smile. "Remember—never fear, Brocket's here!"

He was right. They were together, they could count on each other, and, after all, they *were* the Detective Mystery Squad! A renewed sense of determination took hold, and Fairday gathered her strength. Nothing could come from crying about the situation. They needed to take action now to get her dog, get back home, and solve this mystery.

Lizzy, Marcus, and Fairday tiptoed to the end of the hallway and began to descend the grand staircase. Stepping onto the black-and-white-checkered floor, they turned around, taking in the foyer. The chandelier sparkled overhead as rainbows shifted in the glow of its light. To their right stood a closed door.

"That's the sitting room," Fairday said, pointing to it. "My mom's working on that room right now. I only got a peek at it before she closed it off."

"Let's take a look, then," Marcus replied, shifting his backpack on his shoulders and moving closer. "It'll be interesting to see what it looks like on this side."

"What if the red-haired lady is in there?" Fairday asked, her eyes flicking from Marcus to the closed door.

"Well," Marcus replied, "we'll probably have to face her sooner or later . . . might as well be sooner."

"I guess you're right," Fairday said as she twisted the end of her ponytail.

She opened the door a crack, and they peered inside. Wow, if her mother could see this! Everything was gleaming; hints of gold and silver shimmered against the glow from several fancy lamps, which stood on wooden end tables. Paintings of colorful landscapes hung from the walls all around them. A fire crackled in a stone hearth with a magnificent mantelpiece strewn with expensive-looking trinkets. Bookshelves lined one side of the room, reaching all the way to the top of the high ceiling, and numerous vases with long-stemmed roses were scattered about.

"Do you guys think this is where the dried rose petals I found on the third floor came from?" Fairday asked.

"Definitely. Whoever it was carried them over from here," Lizzy replied.

Fairday pulled open the door a bit wider, and they moved inside. Marcus quickly scanned it with his infrared goggles and nodded that the coast was clear. Walking around, Fairday was trying very hard not to touch anything but found it nearly impossible. Marcus was already rolling a strange-looking blue glass ball between the palms of his hands, and Lizzy was lifting a sparkling figurine off the bookshelf. Fairday's friend was like a crow when it came to shiny things.

"I don't think we should touch anything. I mean, what if she comes in here and finds us messing around with her stuff?" Fairday peered at Lizzy and Marcus, who sheepishly looked back at her. Lizzy immediately slid the trinket back onto its shelf, and Marcus set down the glass ball.

"You're right. We are, after all, uninvited guests." Lizzy sighed, staring at the dazzling treasure.

Fairday looked forlornly at the wall of books and hoped she'd get to read them on the other side of the house. Suddenly, they heard a knock and immediately turned to face the door. It was still open a crack, but next to it they noticed a large orb resting in a metal frame. The globe began to glow with white smoke swirling around inside. Walking over, they were startled to see Mr. Morrow opening the front door of Fairday's house for some painters.

"Oh my gosh," Lizzy whispered. "This must be a window into what's happening on the other side."

"How do you think it works?" Fairday asked.

"No knobs or buttons," Marcus added, checking it out.

After gazing at it for a few minutes, they realized the only view it gave was of the front door. "I guess it just shows who's coming into and going out of the house. It's scary to think how many places there are on this side where you can spy on my family on the other side," Fairday said, biting her lip.

"Yeah. Well, at least things seem to be moving along as they were before we went through the mirror," Lizzy replied.

Turning back to face Marcus and Fairday, she continued. "I guess we should go and check out the kitchen next to see if Auntie Em's in there. What do you guys think?"

Marcus and Fairday nodded in agreement, and they all turned to head out the door. Just then, the glass ball that Marcus had been playing with rolled off the table and plummeted to the ground, the sound of breaking glass shattering the silence that had enveloped them since they arrived.

# TWENTY-FIVE

## A TERRIFYING TWIST

The DMS stood rooted to the spot, no one daring to take a breath as they waited and listened. Not a sound could be heard, so they quietly marched toward the kitchen.

Fairday was impressed to see all of the appliances gleaming. She swiveled her head, taking in her surroundings, and her eyes settled on the stove. The clock was not foggy, but it read three o'clock, just like on the other side of the mirror! She wasn't sure what that meant, but her fingers itched to write it down in her notebook. *Time stopped at the same moment on this side too!* Suddenly, a long sour note burst out from behind them and sent the DMS jumping into the air, grabbing for each other's arms.

"What was that?" Lizzy whispered, her eyes widening.

"The bagpipes," Fairday whispered back. "What should we do?"

"We have to go out there and see what's going on. We'll never get to the bottom of this if we run away," Marcus said, his confidence winning him Fairday's vote. "And we have that water bottle. Who knows? We could luck out like Dorothy."

Nodding in agreement, they took a united step into the foyer. Another note rang out; it sounded like it was coming from under the grand staircase. Inching her way forward, Fairday thought she noticed something green glinting in the dark. Marcus had on his night-vision goggles and began pointing excitedly to the dark space under the stairs.

"There's someone there!" Marcus whispered as a pair of emerald eyes emerged from out of the blackness. Fairday's shriek of terror reverberated off the walls as the group backed up and pivoted on their heels. They ran full throttle up the staircase, shoving and pushing each other as they tried to make their escape.

A screech echoed through the house, followed by a raspy voice that shouted, "STOP!"

"Hurry, hurry, hurry," Fairday chanted as they ran. With a glance over her shoulder, she saw a tangled mane of wild, red hair streaking up the staircase after them. "Oh God! Oh God! She's right behind us!" she belted out in gasps, forcing her legs to pump up and down even harder. Marcus was in the lead, bounding up the staircase with Lizzy just behind him.

"STOP!" the voice repeated. It sounded maniacal and very, very close. Fairday imagined feeling the crazed woman's hot breath breathing down the back of her neck as she leaped over the top step.

"Yeah, right! I'm sure you just want to invite us for tea and pastries or something!" Marcus hollered over his shoulder.

They rocketed down the second-floor corridor, backpacks banging into each other. Finally, they made it to the door and stopped, looking back to get a quick glimpse of their attacker.

A rush of wind hit their faces as the ghastly pursuer flew down the corridor at them. "AH!" Fairday screamed, fumbling to get through the door.

"Open it!" Lizzy yelled.

Suddenly, Marcus threw down his pack and ran straight at the blur of red speeding toward them. His fists were held high out in front of him and his eyes were on fire.

"Marcus, what . . . ?" Lizzy yelled, but before she could get out the words, Marcus stopped; he was frozen in place, his eyes the only things moving as they bulged out of their sockets, staring wildly at the sight before him. It was as if his body had been turned into a wax statue. Lizzy and Fairday continued to back themselves against the door.

"Where's Auntie Em? What do you want from us?"

Fairday shouted, her voice shaking. Panicking, she clasped the water bottle and chucked it at the lady. There was a thud as the bottle bounced off its target. *Rats! It wasn't open!* Now, even the possibility of using water as a defense was gone.

A crazed laugh escaped the lips of the terrifying woman standing in front of them. Her red hair slithered around her face like serpents being wooed by a snake charmer. Two hands reached out and grabbed for Fairday, the woman's bony fingers squeezing into her arms. Opening her mouth to scream, Fairday found that nothing would come out. She'd lost her voice.

Lizzy reacted fast, hurling her DMS pack hard at the woman's head and yelling at the top of her lungs, "LET HER GO, YOU PSYCHO!" The backpack soared through the air, heading straight for its target. But just as it was about to strike, it, too, froze in midair and then fell limply to the floor. Lizzy tried to attack but suffered the same fate. She stood frozen, except for her eyes, which were frantically shifting back and forth.

As Fairday hung inches from the floor, her heart was pounding in her chest. The red-haired woman held her up, squeezing her arms painfully to her sides. She was a breath away from her captor's face. The deranged woman's large pupils pulsed like black holes attempting to suck her soul into their depths.

# TWENTY-SIX

## A FLASH IN THE DARK

Fairday's eyes were open, but everything was dark. She could hear Lizzy breathing hard next to her, and a moan came from somewhere to her left.

"Marcus?" Fairday called out, reaching around for him blindly. "Where are you? Say something." She felt panicked as her fingers pushed through tufts of soft patches strewn about on the floor.

"Uh," Lizzy moaned. "What's going on? Where are we?" Her voice was weak.

"I don't know," Fairday replied shakily as her hands finally fell upon Marcus. "Are you okay?"

"Ooow," he groaned. "Wha ... Where's this?" Fairday

felt him move upright into a sitting position. "Why's it so dark?"

"Wait!" Lizzy said, causing Marcus and Fairday to jump. "Ugh, I was going to turn on my headlamp, but it's gone."

"My goggles are missing too! My dad's gonna kill me," Marcus said.

Muffled fumbling came from Lizzy's direction. "Aha! Yes, I have it!"

"Have what?" Fairday asked.

"The camera. I put it in my pocket earlier," Lizzy said. "I can use the flash to take a picture; then we can at least get an idea of where we are."

There was a click, and a flash of light illuminated their surroundings, leaving ghostly traces floating through the blackness. Fairday could feel Marcus slide in next to her as Lizzy brought the picture up.

They huddled together over the camera as the picture on the viewer appeared. Three faces lit up from the glow of the lights, and they all leaned in to get a better look at what it had captured. In the picture, right next to Fairday's head, something long and thin hung in midair, a metallic shimmer glinting off it.

"There's something hanging next to your head, Fairday," Lizzy said.

What could be hanging from the ceiling? Could it be a trap? Fairday squeezed her eyes closed, bracing herself for the worst, and reached above her. Her fingers touched what felt like a long cord. Taking a deep breath, she yanked it.

Soft yellow light flooded the room. It was a chain attached to a lightbulb, which hung down from the ceiling and flickered as it swung back and forth above their heads.

The room they were in was small and dusty. *Ah,* thought Fairday, *dust bunnies.* Those must have been the soft patches she had felt. There was only one other object in the room. "The world's oldest mop and bucket!" she shouted. "They still look the same."

"Huh?" Marcus said.

"This is the closet across from my bedroom!" Fairday said as she jiggled the handle. "She's locked us in here."

"Ugh! Our packs are gone!" Lizzy replied, stomping her foot. "Well, luckily we're all in one piece."

The DMS looked at each other, trying to assess their situation. *At least we aren't in the dark anymore,* thought Fairday. The unsteady beam of light gave her a glimmer of hope.

"How did we get in here? The last thing I remember was some force stopping me in my tracks; then everything went blank," Lizzy said.

"Yeah," Marcus said. "Everything went blank for me, too, like somebody shut off a switch in my head." He reached up and touched his hair, as if he were actually going to find some kind of on/off switch he wasn't aware of. "What'd she do to you, Fairday?"

"Well, first I threw the closed water bottle at her, which didn't quite have the effect I was going for." Fairday smirked.

"If I hadn't been so scared, I would've burst out laughing," Lizzy chuckled.

"Of course, I missed the whole thing," Marcus said. "My switch was off."

"I can't believe I did that. Anyway, then she held me up close to her face. It was so scary—her eyes looked like black holes." Fairday shivered at the memory. "Everything was happening so fast, and then it just stopped. The next thing I remember is opening my eyes, and it was dark."

"How can she do that? I mean, is she a witch or something?" Lizzy asked. "It's so creepy how her hair can move by itself. Ugh! She does look like the red-haired lady in the picture. Only, you know, really scary instead of clever and fancy. So it's possible the lady we saw in the mirror and this one are the same. They both must be Ruby Begonia. Maybe she's just different on this side. That's who we're dealing with, right?"

"Or," Fairday said, "it could be someone disguised as her."

"But why would someone disguise themselves as her and live in this weird place?" Marcus said. "It just doesn't make any sense."

"Well, whoever she is, we're bound to find out. One thing's for certain—she's got her sneaker back," Lizzy said. "Along with all the other evidence we've collected so far."

# TWENTY-SEVEN

## A GOOD PLACE TO HIDE

The DMS sat cross-legged in a circle on the floor, trying to think of a way out of the closet.

"Okay," Lizzy said. "The door's locked, so we can't get out that way, unless one of you knows how to pick a lock." She looked up at Marcus and Fairday.

"Actually, I do. My dad taught me about locking mechanisms," Marcus replied. Fairday's heart lifted, then instantly fell as he added, "But I would need something small and sharp in order to do it like a bobby pin."

All Fairday had on her was the elastic she tied her hair back with, which clearly wasn't going to do any good. If only they had their DMS packs. There were all sorts of tools zipped up in them. Lizzy's brother's multitool key chain came to mind.

"Yes!" Lizzy blurted out, then stood up and shoved her hand into the back pocket of her jeans. She pulled out a bobby pin and handed it to Marcus. "I always keep a spare bobby pin on me in case I want to put my hair back," she stated, flipping her springy curls away from her face.

"Now we're in business!" Marcus said, grabbing it from Lizzy and moving toward the closet door.

They watched as he finagled the bobby pin into the key-hole and began jiggling it around. It seemed like forever until, finally, there was a click and the lock popped.

The door slowly opened and they peered out. "All clear," Fairday whispered.

"Let's go," Lizzy replied, and they sneaked into the hall-way.

Carefully they made their way to the door at the end that led to the third floor. "What about Auntie Em? Oh, I hope she's okay! And what about our DMS packs?" Fairday asked, stopping just before they were about to head up the stairs. "We can't leave them here. I need my dog, and we need our stuff!"

"We have to find a way back to the other side," Marcus said. "We can come back for them once we know how to get in and out of this place."

"I think Marcus is right," Lizzy said, noticing the look on Fairday's face. "I mean, once we know how to get back, then at least we'll know how to save Auntie Em and get away from Batty Begonia if she comes after us again."

Fairday smiled faintly at Lizzy's nickname for the lunatic they were running from. "Okay. You guys are right. Let's get outta here."

Up the spiral staircase and through the archway they crept. "The mirror's still like a window," Lizzy noted as she approached it and touched the cool glass. "Hey! There's the brass key." She pointed to it hanging from the lock on the balcony door on the other side. "What should we do?"

"I wish we still had it. Then we could try using it on this side. If only we'd thought to grab the key," Fairday said, frustrated.

"Well, um, maybe it slipped our minds because we were being attacked by a freaky willow tree. Don't beat yourself up, Fairday. None of us thought of it," Marcus said.

"I guess," she mumbled.

Suddenly, they heard footsteps from below and immediately froze. The sound of a door being flung open echoed through the house.

"NOOOOOO!" bellowed the crazy Begonia lady.

"What do we do? Where should we go?" Fairday looked around for someplace to hide.

"There!" Lizzy pointed to her right, and they bolted into the third-floor room.

They shut the door as quietly as possible. They could hear stomping footsteps heading up the spiral staircase as they tried to find a place to hide.

"Over here!" Lizzy said in a frenzied whisper, racing across the room. She stood before the wardrobe, poised to knock. "Oh, oh, what's the code to open it?"

Marcus looked dumbfounded, but Fairday knew exactly what Lizzy was up to. "Knock thrice and three to open the door, knock thrice and four to lock it once more!" she exclaimed, thrilled she'd remembered the sequence. Lizzy knocked in fast repetitions: one, two, three . . . one, two, three, and the iron claws unclenched.

Without a sound, they opened the wardrobe doors and piled in, quickly pulling them closed. Fairday held them shut as Lizzy softly knocked—one, two, three . . . one, two, three, four—and the claws clasped together on the other side just as the door to the third-floor room banged open.

# TWENTY-EIGHT

## A SHIFT IN DIRECTION

Pressing their ears against the wardrobe, they waited in anticipation. After several minutes of silence, Fairday whispered, "Should we check to see if she's out there?"

"I suppose. We can't sit in here all day," Lizzy said. "I'll have to knock, though, which will point her in our direction if she's waiting for us."

"Just do it," Marcus replied. "We'll have to find out who's out there eventually."

"All right, then," Lizzy said, and knocked three times plus three. The door unlatched and she pushed it open a crack.

Three sets of eyes, striking gray, deep brown, and bright blue, peered into the room. Suddenly, Fairday flung open the double doors. "I don't believe it! It's a portal!" she gasped. "We're back!"

Quickly exiting the wardrobe, the DMS emerged into the familiar surroundings of the boxes filled with junk.

"What do you guys think we should do?" Lizzy asked.

Fairday thought for a moment. "Well, the good part in all of this is we now know how to get in and out of the other side, and . . ." She paused, turning to face the door to the room. "Remember, the brass key is right out there. Wait a sec." She bounded out of the room and returned with it hanging around her neck.

"Good call," Lizzy noted, glancing at the key.

Marcus crossed his arms over his chest and said, "I think we should look for more clues. Why is this weird woman haunting your house and taking your stuff? At least on this side we can poke around uninterrupted."

"Yeah, I agree," Lizzy said as she plopped down on the chair. "There must be something here that explains what's going on. I mean, look around. There's so much stuff in these boxes that belonged to the Begonias. I know we've already checked out most of it, but maybe we missed something."

"What if there are instructions for the mirror or the wardrobe?" Marcus asked. "Too bad we can't look up the information on the Internet or just call a store or something."

"Yeah, right. Thurston Begonia bought that old mirror

and the freaky wardrobe off the Internet, which didn't even exist then. I think you should have fallen harder down the stairs, Marcus, to fix your brain," Lizzy said, smirking at him.

"Just thinking out loud, smarty pants," he replied. "What I'm saying, if someone will let me finish, is we should start checking out the evidence in here first."

"Wait! There may not be instructions for the mirror or the wardrobe, but we know there might be magical blue-prints for the house hidden someplace. Those could be very helpful!" Fairday said.

Marcus and Lizzy moved to different corners of the room and began searching. Noticing the broken doll star-ing up at her, Fairday bent down to look through the rest of the box. Other than some fancy teacups, the creepy doll was the only interesting item. Looking up, she saw Lizzy crouched down, peering under the wardrobe.

Suddenly, Marcus shouted, "Hey! Have you already sorted through this box marked 'bills'?"

Shaking their heads, they both replied, "Nope."

Marcus began sifting through the papers. The girls walked over and each took a stack. After a few minutes, he blurted out, "Yes! I found something!" Grinning, Marcus waved a piece of paper in the air to grab the girls' attention.

"What'd you find?" Lizzy asked.

"Check this out! It's a letter, and it's addressed to Ruby," he said.

"Another one?" Fairday asked. Their evidence was hidden in the oddest places.

The three detectives knelt together, reading the letter:

My Dearest Ruby,

I am sorry every day for what I have done to you. It all began when I was attacked by outlaws while traveling through the Black Forest in Germany. I wandered through the woods for days until I came upon a shack in the middle of a swamp. There I met a gypsy named Eldrich. She gave me shelter and then pointed me in the right direction. Before I left, she sold me a glass orb, claiming that if I ever spoke her name into it, she would appear and grant me a wish, at a price, of course.

Fairday shot Marcus a quick glance as she recalled the blue glass ball that had rolled off the table and shattered into a million pieces. Could that have been what had broken? Marcus's expression was one of pure innocence. She smiled, her eyes shifting back to the letter.

The blueprints you found were designed by Eldrich for your mother. She was always so sick, and I loved her with all my heart. All I wanted was to take her to safety on the other side of the mirror, which is an enchanted parallel world. My plan was that after you were born, the three of us would be together forever. When the gypsy's magic failed and I couldn't save your mother, I refused to pay Eldrich's price. Her revenge on me was taken out on you, and for this I have lost everything.

Fairday's mind skipped to the shadow hidden behind the willow in the picture Lizzy had sent her. That must have been Eldrich spying on the happy couple. Looking down, she finished reading the letter.

Once I saw the brass key in the balcony door, I was sure Eldrich had somehow collected the debt I owed her and tricked you into going into the mirror. To make matters worse, I can no longer use the magic of the house or I would have come to you by now. I am sure Eldrich placed some sort of curse on me so I cannot access the magic. I only hope one day the curse will be lifted, and I will get to see you again. Please forgive me. I would do anything to take it all back.

"So Larry Lovell was right. There was a curse on the Begonias. I wonder if Ruby's been trapped in there since she went missing on her wedding day," Fairday said, folding up the letter and slipping it into her pocket.

"That must be what happened. And now we know Thurston wished for the blueprints," Marcus said. "We *have* to find them!"

"Maybe we're not looking in the right places," Lizzy said. "I think it's time to look somewhere else."

"There are a million rooms in this house," Fairday said, sounding vexed. "I wouldn't even know where to start."

"I have an idea," Marcus said.

"What is it?" Lizzy asked, looking hopeful.

"You're not gonna like it, but I think we should check out the willow tree. Who knows? It's magical, and there could be something that points us in the right direction." He motioned out the window to the backyard.

"But what if it comes alive and tries to attack us again?" Fairday said, her voice quavering.

"Hmmm," muttered Lizzy, watching Marcus with interest. "He might be right. There could be a hidden clue, and I think we should give it a try."

They pounded down the stairs, navigating their way through the workers and paint cans. A radio was blaring as the remodeling continued.

"Fairday! Can you come here for a minute?" Mr. Morrow called out from the kitchen.

"What's up, Dad?" Fairday asked as she approached him, panting slightly and looking over her shoulder at her partners, who were both waiting anxiously by the door.

"I tried looking for you before, but you kids must have been outside."

"Oh, we were taking Auntie Em for a walk," she said, thinking fast on her feet. Fairday didn't want to alert her dad to the fact that their dog was missing.

"All right. Just an FYI. Mom's going to be working late with the contractors, so it's just us for dinner, which will be around seven. You can invite your new friend if you want." He looked over at Marcus.

"Um, okay. Thanks, Dad. What time is it now?" Fairday asked, realizing she had absolutely no concept of what time it was or how long they had been gone.

Mr. Morrow checked his watch. "Quarter to five."

"Okay, see you at dinner. We'll be in and out until then. Lots to explore!" Fairday grinned. Rushing over to her friends, she said, "Thank goodness there's so much activity around here. My dad didn't even really notice we were gone. It's almost five, which means we were on the other side for about an hour."

"So it seems that time passes normally in the real world, even though it's stopped on the other side," Marcus said as they crossed the backyard, heading for the willow tree.

"Yeah, and I'm pretty sure the other Begonia House is stuck at three o'clock on the day Ruby disappeared," Lizzy surmised. "So the two houses are connected in that moment, with the other house trapped in the past and ours in the present."

"What about her, though?" Marcus asked. "If Ruby was trapped in there since her wedding day, we need to find out why. Maybe she didn't want to get married or she was mad at her father? And how does she have those magical powers? You know, like putting us into a trance and making her hair move by itself?" He turned to Lizzy and Fairday, raising his eyebrows.

Lizzy responded, gesturing for emphasis. "These are the questions we need to find the answers to, and we need to find them fast. Remember, Old Batty Begonia knows how to get in and out of the mirror without the brass key. She was able to coerce Margo and Auntie Em into it, and, Fairday, you saw the door in the mirror the first day you moved in."

"Yeah." Fairday *had* seen the door in the mirror, and red shoes stepping back through it. "But I didn't actually see her come out of there. Maybe Margo saw the sneakers in the mirror and went after them. I mean, you know, Margo's not exactly shy. And *maybe* because she's a baby, the laws of reality don't apply to her. She didn't seem to think there was anything strange about crawling through a mirror and pulling out a sneaker covered in jewels. Auntie Em's a dog—who knows how the magic works with animals?"

"I think you're right about the baby thing, because how else could Margo hear us through the painting?" Lizzy asked.

"But," Marcus said, "you've been hearing bagpipe music since the first day you moved in. So she had to have been on this side when she was playing it. You wouldn't have been able to hear it if she had been playing on the other side. Remember, your mom couldn't hear you yelling from the other side of the painting. I'd bet a million bucks that Old Bats knows about the wardrobe."

"Marcus is right. I mean, we figured it out," Lizzy replied.

"By accident, though," Fairday said, twisting the end of her ponytail. Some lunatic could invade her house whenever they felt like it, whether she wanted to believe it or not.

"Yeah, it was an accident, but I'm sure she's figured out that little trick," Marcus said. "It's great that we discovered it, but she probably uses the wardrobe all the time."

"Okay, now I definitely want to move back to the city," Fairday said, giving Marcus and Lizzy an uneasy smile. She'd certainly had enough haunting to last her a lifetime.

"What!" Marcus exclaimed. "And miss out on all this? Now, that would be crazy!" He nudged her jokingly as they continued walking across the barren backyard.

Lizzy, Marcus, and Fairday slowed their pace as they came upon the willow. The tree stood before them, towering above their heads. Its twisted branches swayed ominously back and forth, creaking and groaning unpleasantly as they shifted in the breeze.

# TWENTY-NINE

## A FORTUNATE FIND

Standing underneath the willow's gnarled branches, Fairday looked up through the tangled web of dead leaves and twisted bark. The tree seemed to stretch right up to the skyline and felt very intimidating from where they were standing.

"Gives me the creeps," Lizzy murmured.

"Sure does," Marcus agreed. "Look at this thing. It must be at least a hundred years old."

Fairday began to move around the trunk, running her fingers over its rough surface. "In that picture, Eldrich was standing right here." She stopped and glanced back at Lizzy and Marcus.

"Yeah, that's the spot," Lizzy confirmed. "Do you see anything? Check around the base."

"No, uh . . ." Fairday bent down and searched the ground; then her eyes began moving up the tree as she scrutinized the bark. "Maybe there's initials or something carved into it?"

"Good thinking," Lizzy replied. After a moment, she asked, "Anything?"

"There!" Fairday shouted. She pointed to a dark knot in the trunk a few feet above her head. "I can see something sticking out."

"Here." Marcus ran forward and knelt down on all fours. "Climb up on my back."

Fairday positioned herself and stood on top of Marcus. Finding her balance, she reached up and pulled herself onto a sturdy branch. Fairday extended her arms as far as possible and felt her fingers brush against something metallic. Risking tiptoes gave her just enough height to make a grab for the object. With one fell swoop, she had it in her hands. "Got it!" she yelled, stepping off the branch onto Marcus's back and jumping to the ground.

"A silver canister! Just like in the diary. Do you think it's the blueprints?" Lizzy asked excitedly.

After trying to pry the stopper out of the canister, they finally got it. Fairday pulled out the contents and held them up for Marcus and Lizzy to see. The package contained several long scrolls, which were held together with a strip of twine. She knelt on the ground and untied it, then unrolled the pages.

"I don't believe it! The blueprints!" Fairday gasped, looking at her partners in amazement.

They all leaned in to get a closer look. "This is fantastic!" Lizzy clapped her hands with glee as she examined the papers now stretched out in the middle of their small circle. There were five sheets in all. Each revealed not only the measurements and dimensions of the house and its grounds, but also the handwritten words Ruby had talked about, wrapped around the edges of the pages. They seemed to be instructions phrased in rhyming riddles.

"Look at this one," Marcus said, pointing to the first page, which showed the front of the house. Underneath the drawing of the entranceway was an inscription. He read the words out loud: "'If a foe seeks to find a way in, and your wish is to never see them again, just speak your mind to the front door, and your enemies shall haunt you no more.'"

"And listen to this!" Lizzy said, leaning over the third page. "'When quiet cannot be found, ring a bell to silence all sound.'"

They flipped through the pages, trying to take it all in. Each page was covered with the phrases, which encircled the sketches of the rooms, the grounds, and even the front gate. Fairday's eyes shifted to the writing underneath the drawing of the gate. "'Close these gates and find yourself protected, but remember, for all those who pass, fear not the unexpected.'" *Whoever wrote that sure wasn't kidding,* Fairday thought.

It seemed that every part of the Begonia House had some magical attribute to it. There were instructions on how to make rooms disappear at will and how to instantly hide unpleasant smells.

When Fairday read, *The rooms can easily change their size; walls will move before your eyes. Just say "voilà" with a flip of hand, and settle your mind on small or grand,* she realized what she had said that made the walls in the third-floor room shift. *It wasn't my imagination!* She really needed to start trusting her instincts more. Fairday wished she could tell her mother about that particular feature, because it would definitely make the renovations easier if her mom could ask a wall to shrink or stretch.

On the fourth page, Fairday found what they were looking for. She pronounced each word slowly: "'If in this place you wish to stay forever, to never age, nor in time wither, there is a door that you can't see; if you want to find it, just use the key.'" Underneath the words, there was a drawing of the brass key and a sketch of the mirror.

The wind began to pick up and caught the corner of the page Fairday was trying to read. "Let's get inside," she said, rolling up the blueprints. Rising to their feet, Lizzy and Marcus nodded in agreement.

Heading back to the house, Fairday suddenly shrieked in terror as she pointed up at the balcony. "Look, up there!"

A horrible face, partially obscured by wispy strands of long grayish hair, was watching them from above. Two skeletal hands slid onto the railing as the figure leaned over the edge and let out a terrifying cackle. Fairday could almost feel the black eyes gazing down at them. Its lips spread into a sneer as it turned and disappeared into the house.

# ~ THIRTY ~

## AN AWKWARD SILENCE

"Who was that?" Marcus blurted out. "Just how many freakos are running around this place?"

"Oh!" Fairday shouted, grabbing for Lizzy's arm. "Whoever that was is in the house with my family. We've got to do something! Auntie Em's already been dog-napped. What if they try to take Margo next? Or . . . or . . . ," she stammered, feeling panicked as she rambled off her worst nightmares, "or what if whoever that was tries to kill my mom or dad?"

"That's not going to happen," Lizzy said, squaring her shoulders. Poking the canister, she added, "Besides, we found these, and assuming the spells work, the house is on *our* side now." She grabbed Fairday's hand and gave it a tight squeeze. "We're going to figure this out."

The DMS hesitated as they approached the entrance of the Begonia House. As Fairday opened the front door, they quietly peered in. The hairs on the back of her neck stood up as she flashed back to the day she and her parents had stood in the same spot. It had seemed foreboding then. Now she knew that all those spooky feelings had been spot on.

This time, the house was not quiet. It was bustling with people and sounds. Fairday could hear squabbling voices in the room to their right. A radio was still playing in the background, and she could hear the contractors humming along to it as they banged their equipment. Rising above it all was the melodious voice of Margo echoing down to them, "OH! DUCKY, DUCKY, NO BATH! UCKY!"

"I guess she doesn't want a bath," Fairday said with a smirk and a shrug of her shoulders.

"Well, at least everything seems normal," Lizzy said.

"It sure does," Marcus agreed. "It's so hard to imagine some creepy person sneaking around in here with all this activity."

"Do you think whoever was on the balcony is waiting for us upstairs? I mean, it's only been a few minutes," Fairday worried.

"Could be," Lizzy mumbled.

While climbing the grand staircase, Fairday said, "Wait! I have an idea!" She quickly turned back and bent down to grab something off the floor. Then she hurtled up the steps, taking them two at a time right to the top, where she knelt down in the hallway. She pulled the blueprints out of the canister and unrolled them on the floor.

"What are you doing?" Marcus asked, leaning over her shoulder to see what was happening. Lizzy knelt down beside her with a puzzled expression.

Fairday held up one of Margo's abandoned toys: a pink plastic ball with yellow stars painted on it.

"What's that for?" Marcus asked, eyeing the object in her hand. Fairday shook it lightly and it jingled.

"Ah!" Lizzy said, and then repeated the words she had read on page three of the blueprints. "If quiet cannot be found, ring a bell to silence all sound!" Her voice rose in excitement as she added, "Good thinking! Let's see if it works!"

Standing in the middle of the hallway, Fairday said the words under her breath, raised the ball into the air, and gave it a good shake. The bell inside tinkled merrily.

Silence enveloped them. It was as if a thick cloud had settled over the house. All of the background noise was gone. Fairday opened her mouth to speak, but nothing came out. Lizzy's expression was one of bewilderment as she held her hand up, trying to touch her own soundless words.

Dropping to his knees, Marcus began scanning the blueprints. Fairday knew he was trying to find a way to undo the spell. It was, after all, very unsettling to open your mouth to say something and have nothing come out. He flipped the page over and pointed to a phrase written in a corner. Fairday and Lizzy leaned in to read the words: *If it's noise you wish to hear once more, stamp your foot, then slam a door.*

Without hesitation, Marcus hurried over to the nearest room and stamped his foot on the floor. He then flung open the door and slammed it closed. The busy sounds of the house filled the air once again.

"Well, it definitely works," Fairday said to her friends, breathing a gigantic sigh of relief that she could hear the words spilling out of her mouth as usual.

"Yeah, it does," Marcus replied, his cheeks flushed. "As freaked out as I was, that was cool!" He looked electrified at this new turn of events. "How much do you want to try out the rest of these?" He tossed the blueprints back to Fairday, and she stuffed them into the canister.

"No time for that now," Lizzy chimed in. "We've got a case to solve."

"Lizzy's right. I can't live here knowing there's a crazy person on the loose." Fairday paused, then added gravely, "More than one, actually."

Making their way down the hallway, Lizzy stopped at the portrait of Cora Lynn Begonia and gazed into her painted eyes.

"Can you see anything?" Fairday asked.

"No, nothing. We'll have to look at the blueprints later and figure out how these things work."

They moved on to the door at the end of the hall. But before they started up the spiral staircase, Marcus stopped. "Okay, so what's the plan?"

"I think we should go back in, get Auntie Em, and try to find our packs. We can bring the blueprints with us to the other side," Lizzy said.

"What if they don't work there?" Fairday asked. "We'll be defenseless against Old Bats again. Probably end up back in the closet. We still have no idea how she managed to put us into that trance."

"We'll just have to take our chances and see. Besides, we know how to get out of the closet, thanks to my curly hair and Marcus's helpful brilliance," Lizzy countered, smiling at her. "I mean, what else can we do? We have to go back in, get your dog and our DMS packs and figure out a plan to stop her from haunting this house!"

"True. But what should we do if she starts chasing us?" Fairday asked, wishing she was as brave as her best friend.

"We should try to find Ruby Begonia first. Then maybe *we* can trap *her*," Marcus said.

"How the heck are we going to trap her? And what about the other person that's wandering around in here? We have no idea who that was, but they certainly did *not* look friendly," Lizzy said.

"I don't know. I guess we'll just have to see what happens," Marcus replied. Once again, they climbed up the spiral staircase, none of them knowing what awaited them.

# THIRTY-ONE

## TOO CLOSE FOR COMFORT

As they neared the top step, their pace slowed while they paused to listen for any indication of trouble. Fairday strained her ears, but it all seemed quiet and calm. Still, she knew she had to keep her wits about her as they proceeded single file through the open archway. Marcus was in the lead, and as he rounded the corner, he blurted out, "Oh my gosh!" Fairday's heart skipped a beat, her stomach twisting into a knot at the tone of his voice. What had just happened?

Lizzy was fast on his heels, blocking Fairday's view. "Auntie Em! Our packs!" she exclaimed. Her eyes widened, and she instinctively ran forward to retrieve them.

"Stop! It's probably a trap!" Marcus yelled, grabbing her sleeve.

Auntie Em sat tied to their backpacks, looking frightened. Fairday's heart ached for her dog. It seemed like everything was right there. Upon further scrutiny, however, she realized they were actually in front of the door reflected on the *other side* of the mirror. *Tricky,* Fairday thought.

"You're right. Sorry," Lizzy muttered. "I wasn't thinking, and I really need to start looking before I leap."

"It seems like it'd be so easy to just grab them," Fairday said forlornly.

"Yeah, but remember—some things are too good to be true," Lizzy replied. "I think Marcus is right. This is way too easy. It has to be a setup. I bet she's just waiting on the other side, and as soon as we try to take them, BAM! She'll appear in the mirror and grab us or put us into another trance."

"Or the willow's branches are already waiting for us," Fairday added. "And as soon as we open the door, they'll throw us off the balcony to our deaths. Yeah, you're right. It probably is a trap."

"Should just one of us go through the mirror?" Marcus looked at his friends' worried faces.

"No, I think it's got to be all of us or none of us," Lizzy said. "If she gets one of us trapped, it could take a lifetime for that person to be rescued. We have no idea what she's capable of."

"Agreed," Fairday and Marcus replied.

"We can't go through the mirror because it's the obvious path. What about the wardrobe?" Fairday suggested. "It brought us to this side, but could it go both ways?" She pointed in two different directions, then glanced at Marcus and Lizzy.

"We should try it," Lizzy said, nodding. "I mean, she knows we found out how to get back through the wardrobe. I'm sure she thinks we'll go through the mirror to get our stuff back, which, unfortunately, could be the only way to get to the other side. If the wardrobe does go both ways, and if we're really lucky, she won't suspect that we'd be coming from the other direction, and maybe there's a chance of getting out before she catches us."

"It's definitely worth a shot," Marcus added. "Two of us should run out and grab Auntie Em and the packs, then book it back into the wardrobe. The person who stays behind will be ready to knock. It'll all only take a minute. Plus, once we've gotten everything back, we can devise a plan to trap her," Marcus said.

"Are we ready?" Fairday asked.

"You betcha!" Lizzy replied.

"Definitely," Marcus answered, and then, with a chuckle, added, "This should be fun."

Fairday knocked: one, two, three . . . one, two, three. The claws unlatched, and they climbed into the wardrobe. She placed the canister containing the blueprints onto the wardrobe floor and then pulled the doors closed. Moments later, she knocked again. Holding her breath, they pushed the doors open a crack and noticed the flames from the candles still flickering on the vanity. "Okay, it worked. We're back," Fairday whispered.

It had been decided that Marcus and Fairday would run out, grab Auntie Em and the packs, and then race back. Lizzy would stand in the wardrobe, ready to knock once they were all safely enclosed behind its clenched claws.

"On the count of three," Lizzy whispered as she grabbed the inside handles. "One, two . . . three!"

The doors flew open, and Marcus and Fairday sprang forth, sprinting through the room. Everything was a blur as Fairday hurtled past the bed. Marcus threw open the door,

and they streamed out onto the landing. She had Auntie Em in her arms and the straps of two of the backpacks in her hands before she knew it. Spinning on her heels, she stole a quick glance at Marcus. He was just behind her carrying one of the packs over his shoulder, and right behind him was a tangled mane of red hair. Two hands reached out and grabbed the collar of his shirt.

"AHHHH!" he yelled as he was pulled backward.

"Marcus!" Fairday shouted, trying to stop her feet from continuing forward while holding tightly to Auntie Em.

"Oh God! Marcus," Fairday heard Lizzy cry out from the bedroom. She could picture Lizzy's blue eyes wide with fear and knew her friend's brain was whirring frantically with the decision of whether or not to leave her designated post to help.

He managed to free himself and bolted forward with Fairday in the lead. Once again, she could feel hot breath on the back of her neck, panting in time to her pounding feet.

They jumped into the wardrobe, crashing into the back of it. Lizzy had ahold of the door handles and quickly pulled them closed behind Marcus, Fairday, and Auntie Em. But before she was able to knock, they were forcefully flung open. In an instant, the maniacal woman was in the wardrobe with them. The doors slammed closed, cloaking all five figures in darkness.

# THIRTY-TWO

## ONE AND THE SAME

For a few terrifying moments the wardrobe rattled and banged. Fairday could hear herself screaming as something cold touched her arm. Suddenly, she heard someone knocking and then a click. The handles unlatched and she shoved her full weight against the doors, which burst open, causing the four of them to spill out onto the floor.

When Fairday opened her eyes, forgetting they had been shut tight, Auntie Em was squirming and whimpering in her arms. Marcus and Lizzy were on either side, looking disheveled and breathing in heavy gasps. They stared up in fright at the wardrobe as they watched the figure emerge. Wispy gray strands of hair fell limply in front of cold black eyes darting furiously over the three of them. Bony fingers wrapped around the edges of the wardrobe doors.

Both Fairday and Lizzy instinctively scooted backward at the wretched sight. But Marcus shot up, pointing at the wardrobe authoritatively as he bellowed, "It is my wish that you stop her." He looked confused as she continued to advance on them. Revelation washed over Marcus's face as he added, "I mean, Wardrobe, would you *please* stop her."

Lizzy looked baffled as she watched Marcus. Fairday thought he had momentarily lost his mind, but suddenly, the wardrobe lurched forward with a loud, heavy clunk. Extending its iron fingers, the furniture reached out and clamped down onto the ghost-white arms of their pursuer.

It was now holding the scary woman hostage. She jerked and struggled against the shackles, but to no avail. Finally, the expression on her face fell, and she let out a terrible cry of defeat. Hanging her head, she allowed the wardrobe to support her frail figure. Auntie Em was barking nonstop at the scene, trying to escape from Fairday's arms.

"Whoa! I thought we'd had it for sure!" Marcus said.

"Marcus, that was brilliant!" Lizzy clambered up from the floor and flung her arms around his neck in a quick hug.

"How in the world did you know how to do that?" Fairday asked, trying to calm her dog down.

"I remembered the spell from the blueprints: 'Fortune

find and fortune told, everything is yours to hold. State your wish as the one in charge, and oblige it will, no matter how small nor large. But don't forget to be polite, or choose it may to ignore your plight.' I just figured it meant you could ask a chair nicely to be more comfortable, or be friendly to a lightbulb to get it to turn on, or something. I had no idea it would work like this," he said, gesturing to the bizarre sight. He added boastfully, "See, I told you that you'd be really thankful I came along. Who knew I had a photographic memory in the face of danger? Detective tools are awesome, but a good memory is even better!"

"Great job, Marcus! I must say, you nailed it," Lizzy said, her cheeks turning pink.

"You really are a detective superhero, Marcus Brocket." Fairday grinned. "And I'm definitely glad you're in the DMS."

"I almost forgot to be polite, though," he said.

Auntie Em was still squirming and barking. Not wanting to attract her parents' attention, Fairday quickly walked over to the door, gave her a quick kiss on the head, and shooed her down the stairs. The little pug moved faster than Fairday had ever seen her move before.

"Thank goodness Auntie Em is safe!" Fairday said, walking to her friends.

"I'm so glad we got her back," Lizzy said. "I can't imagine this family without that little drooling sausage."

"She seems okay," Marcus chimed in.

"Auntie Em's fine," Fairday replied, sounding relieved. "I'm sure she'll soon be snoring away somewhere."

They turned their attention to the prisoner. Standing a safe distance away, they began to consider the situation. "That's who we saw on the balcony," Lizzy said in a hushed voice. Fairday could tell Lizzy felt awkward talking right in front of the woman, even if she had been trying to kill them, or capture them, or whatever she had been trying to do.

Marcus replied, "I know it was the red-haired lady who followed us into the wardrobe. They must be one and the same—the lady we think is Ruby Begonia and this thin—uh . . . her," he added uncomfortably.

"I am Ruby Begonia," the voice said in a raspy moan, tears welling up in the corners of her black eyes.

# ~ THIRTY-THREE ~

## THE MISSING PIECE

Fairday noticed something odd reflected in the dark pools of Ruby's eyes. There was a sparkle swimming around amid the two black irises. She glanced down to see where the colors were coming from, then gasped. "Lizzy, look at her feet!"

Lizzy's eyes shot downward. "I don't believe it! She's wearing the sneakers!"

Dangling from under the hem of the tattered blue dress were the ruby- and diamond-covered high-heeled sneakers. The moment seemed to freeze as they all fixated on the shoes. Fairday noticed that something wasn't quite right. When Lizzy had tried the sneaker, it had slid on like Dorothy's ruby slippers, fitting her perfectly. On Ruby, however, both feet appeared to be stuffed into the shoes. Fairday could see the skin around her spindly ankles was swollen, and her toes practically popped out where the white laces were tied up. Peeking at Lizzy, she saw that her friend also looked confused. Why would anyone wear shoes that clearly didn't fit?

Fairday spoke up. "What do you want with us?"

Raising her eyes, Ruby tilted her head to the side and smiled; it was a horrid grin, exposing yellow teeth and blackened gums. "Why, my dears"—her voice was gravelly and cold as she spoke through cracked lips—"I only wanted to talk with you. I've been here alone for so long now."

"Most people who want to have a nice chat don't chase down their guests and throw them into a closet," Marcus said, staring back at her.

Ruby's dark eyes welled up with anguish. "How else was I going to get you to listen to me? Look at me! I'm a monster!"

"Why do you look completely different on the other side?" Lizzy asked, moving a bit closer to her.

"I'm cursed," she whispered, dropping her head again.

"Cursed?" Fairday questioned. "Who cursed you? Eldrich? Does it have something to do with the sneakers?" She didn't know why she went right to the sneakers being the reason for the curse; it just seemed right. Perhaps because she would feel cursed, too, if she had to wear shoes that caused her to have blisters on her heels. They looked so uncomfortable that Fairday involuntarily wiggled her own toes, simply because she could.

"Yes! These damned sneakers are the reason I am what I am now." Ruby kicked out her feet, leaning forward against her restraints, as she spat a disgusting spray of green spittle down at the sparkling shoes.

"Ugh," Lizzy moaned, and quickly turned away. Fairday knew that Lizzy hated the sight of spit, and this particular spit couldn't have possibly been any more disgusting.

Ruby spread out the bony fingers on both of her hands and wiggled them teasingly. "I know you've read my diary but I can tell you the *whole* story, if you want to hear it. That is, if you'd kindly ask the wardrobe to release me."

"I don't think that's a good idea," Fairday said.

Marcus rounded on Ruby. "Yeah, as far as we're concerned, lady, you're a madwoman. You kidnapped Fairday's dog, chased us down, froze us, threw us into a closet, and left us there in the dark. Plus, you've been creeping around this house and spooking Fairday. Why should we believe anything you say?"

"You tried to steal my baby sister!" Fairday said.

"Actually, my dear, *she* stole something from *me*." Ruby let the words hang in the air as she shifted her gaze down and jiggled a foot.

"But . . ." Fairday started to speak and then stopped. That was true. Margo had taken the high-heeled sneaker from her. "Maybe we should get my dad?" was the thought that came out instead. She was feeling unnerved and completely unsure of what to do next.

"Fairday, we can't tell your parents. I mean, how on earth would we explain all of this?" Lizzy said.

"I think we should listen to her story before we decide to tell anyone else," Marcus suggested.

"I don't think we should release her, though," Fairday said, her voice cracking. "I mean, we have no idea what she'll do."

"Ah," he said, smiling. "Once again, I think I have an idea that will help us solve this problem!" He walked up to Ruby Begonia but fixed his stare on the wardrobe. "Okay, Wardrobe, would you please set Ruby Begonia down in that chair in the corner?"

The wardrobe lurched forward, clunking down heavily on the floor, then began to hop over to the chair. Ruby was tossed up and down like a sack of potatoes as it banged its way over. Fairday couldn't help but smile. *Now, that's something you don't see every day,* she thought, noticing Marcus and Lizzy trying to suppress grins.

Just before the wardrobe reached its destination, Marcus spoke up again, this time talking to the chair. "Chair, could you please hold Ruby Begonia in her seat once she sits down?"

The wardrobe shifted on its wooden feet so that Ruby was suspended over the striped chair like a swinging pendulum. Fairday held her breath as it released its grip and dropped her onto the requested target. The second she hit the cushions, the striped ribbons began to twist out of the fabric. They ensnared her arms and legs as they quickly wrapped around her thin body. When it was over, Fairday thought she looked like a bizarre Christmas present tied up neatly with red and black bows.

"Marcus, you've got to be the smartest person alive," Lizzy beamed.

"You really get that spell, don't you?" Fairday added.

"I guess, once you realize the potential, it's all open for experimentation," he said. "I was goi—"

But they never got to hear what Marcus was going to do. He was interrupted by the sound of pounding feet racing up the spiral staircase.

# THIRTY-FOUR

## A QUICK COVER

Fairday reacted fast, running over and snatching a sheet that was crumpled up on the floor. She tossed it to Lizzy, knowing her friend would understand what she wanted her to do with it. Fairday, her heart beating like a runaway train, hoped she would appear calm under the scrutiny of whichever parent awaited her. She had no idea how she was going to keep this whole crazy situation from getting even more out of control.

As she reached the door to the room, she glanced back and saw Lizzy whipping the sheet over Ruby Begonia, hiding her from view. Marcus started shuffling things around noisily, while Lizzy began chattering away in a loud voice. Fairday knew they were trying to make enough ruckus to drown out any sounds their concealed captive might make.

Wiping her palms on her jeans, she grasped the handle and casually opened the door. Stepping out, Fairday pulled the door behind her so that it was open just a crack, then stood directly in front of it. Using every bit of acting ability she possessed, she attempted to appear completely normal as her father rounded the corner. His face was flushed and his hair was a mess.

"Hey, Dad, what's up?" she asked, managing to keep her voice calm, though the words came out slightly faster than usual.

"What is going on up here? Is everyone all right?" he asked, his voice reflecting both concern and annoyance. "I heard banging and who knows what else. I thought someone was hurt! I had images of the floor giving way or . . . something falling on one of you kids." He was breathing hard and his voice was shaking a bit.

"Oh, that." Fairday shrugged, knowing she couldn't lie completely when her dad was clearly this upset. Wanting to ease his mind, she said in her most truthful voice, "Well, we wanted to move the wardrobe to make room for a game"—she shrugged—"or at least, we tried to move it."

"You tried to move that thing? By yourselves?" Mr. Morrow exclaimed. He leaned to the side, trying to peer through the slightly open door.

Fairday shifted her feet and blocked his view. "I know!" she said, trying to sound as believable as possible. "It was way too heavy for us, so it started to teeter a bit. I guess it came down hard on the floor. We had no idea it weighed that much! I guess old furniture can be full of surprises!" She laughed lightly, hoping her dad was buying her story. Well, it was partially true, she reasoned; the wardrobe had moved, and it was full of surprises.

"I don't want you kids moving any more furniture. If you want something moved, let me know," Mr. Morrow said sternly. At that moment, Lizzy let out a completely fake-sounding laugh. Luckily, Mr. Morrow seemed to think nothing of it. He raised an eyebrow at Fairday as he strained to peek once again over her shoulder into the room. Some of the items strewn about were visible through the crack in the door. "I guess everything seems okay in there. Sounds like you're having fun. Hmm, I see most of the boxes have been sorted through," he noted, his voice much more even now. "Well, you can regale me with stories about all the interesting items you've found when we sit down for dinner, which will be served in a little over an hour."

Fairday's heartbeat quickened as his words sank in. They would never have this situation solved in time. She had to stall. Thinking fast, she was struck by the craziest idea. Suddenly, she knew what, or actually who, they needed: Larry Lovell. Throwing caution to the wind, she asked, "Dad, is it all right if I call Mr. Lovell and invite him over for dinner tonight?"

Mr. Morrow's expression was one of bewilderment. She pressed on with her ploy, praying she'd be able to convince him it was a good idea. "You know, the reporter I'm doing my project on? I . . . um . . . he was really intriguing and . . . and I'd really like to get to know him better." *Lame*, she thought. *He's going to know something's up.* Crossing her fingers behind her back, she hoped that her far-fetched plan would play out.

"I don't know, Fairday. We don't want to bother him on a Saturday evening. It's really short notice."

"He told me to call him if I had any more questions, that . . . that he'd be happy to help me," she stammered. If anyone could shed some light on this mystery, it was the man who had written about it. Plus, there was just something about Larry Lovell that she trusted, and he *had* told her to call if she needed his help. "Seriously, Dad, he said I could call him anytime." Fairday gazed pleadingly into her father's eyes.

After a moment's pause, he said, "All right, I guess there's no harm in calling to see if he's free. The more the merrier, I suppose. To be honest, I wouldn't mind hearing some of his stories." Mr. Morrow winked. "I bet he has some pretty unbelievable tales to tell."

Fairday felt her shoulders relax as she realized she had just managed to defuse her father's fears and, in the same breath, buy the DMS a little more time. Giving her dad a peck on the cheek, she thanked him and headed back into the room. Shutting the door behind her, she turned to face her friends. Marcus and Lizzy were waiting anxiously to hear what had happened. She felt confident they would agree with her plan to include Larry Lovell. Either way, she had a phone call to make.

# THIRTY-FIVE

## A CALL FOR HELP

"H'llo?" the familiar, grumbling voice answered four agonizing rings later.

"Mr. Lovell, it's Fairday Morrow," she said with a shaking voice, and it suddenly dawned on her that she had no idea what to say. Would he think she was completely mental if she just blurted out what was going on? Fairday could feel a static energy in his silence and right away knew Larry Lovell understood; something was wrong.

"What is it? Do you need my help, Miss Morrow?" His tone was sharp and alert.

"Yes," she breathed down the line. "It's Ruby Begonia. We . . . I mean, we, um . . . we have her." The words seemed to catch in her throat, as she heard an intake of breath from the other end.

"I'll be right there," he responded. "Wait for me, Miss Morrow, and"—he paused—"beware." She heard a click and the connection was broken.

It was decided that Lizzy and Marcus would remain in the room to keep watch over their prisoner while Fairday waited downstairs for Larry Lovell to arrive. She stood at the top of the grand staircase, shifting from foot to foot while staring down at the double doors. Auntie Em was snoozing in her favorite spot, snoring away as if nothing had happened.

After what seemed like forever, there was a loud knock: *bang, bang, bang.* The pug jolted awake and barked as Fairday flew down the stairs as fast as she could, wanting to make sure she was the one to greet him. She knew if her father got to him first, he would keep Larry Lovell chatting for the rest of the night.

Just as Fairday reached the door, Mr. Morrow popped his head out of the kitchen. Casually wiping his hands on a dish towel, he sauntered over and asked humorously, "Now, who might that be?" He flung open the doors and extended a friendly hand. "Why, hello there! You must be Mr. Lovell."

How was she going to get him away from her father now? Time was ticking, and she knew they wouldn't be able to hold Ruby Begonia for much longer without causing a

scene. *Lizzy and Marcus must be freaking out by now,* she thought as she tried to catch the attention of her visitor.

Larry Lovell was standing in the entrance wearing a long trench coat. His hat was tilted to the side as he leaned on his cane. He reached out and shook Mr. Morrow's hand. Clearing his throat, he grumbled, "Humph. Yes, hello, I'm Larry Lovell." But at that instant, his eyes met Fairday's, and she could see the sharpness of intent twinkling behind his wire-rim glasses.

"Well, Mr. Lovell, it seems my daughter is quite eager to know more about you." Mr. Morrow opened his arms in a welcoming gesture as Larry Lovell walked into the foyer. Fairday couldn't help but notice Mr. Lovell's wide-eyed expression as he took in the old house. "Why don't you come and sit down? Dinner won't be ready for a little while, but I can certainly brew up some coffee while you fill us in on—"

Larry immediately interrupted in a very grandfatherly voice. "Hmph, hmph. Mr. Morrow, thank you for inviting me over. I would love to sit and chat with you and your family."

Fairday's heart sank at his words. Was it possible she had been wrong about him? Their entire plan relied wholly upon the belief that somehow, he knew they needed him. Hadn't he cautioned her on the phone when she told him they had Ruby Begonia? Desperate to get him alone, she was about to blurt out something like "Dad, can I show him my bedroom?" which would sound totally absurd and surely blow her cover. But to her relief, he quickly added, "Actually, if it's all right with you, sir, I would love for this young lady here to give me a tour. I have always found this home to be quite fascinating." His eyes crinkled at the corners as he smiled up at Mr. Morrow.

Mr. Morrow unconsciously ran his hands through his messy black hair, clearly trying to decide whether it was a good idea. Finally, he shrugged and in a light voice said, "Well, okay, why not? The construction's done for today, so go ahead, Fairday. Give 'im the grand tour." He glanced up at Larry's hat, adding, "Would you like me to hang up your hat for you?"

"Nope, if that's all right." Larry tapped his hat, then mumbled, "Never take it off if I can help it. Cold air gets into my noggin, and I'm shiverin' all night. Besides, I don't like people goggling at my bald head."

Fairday smirked. He really did seem like such a surly fellow, but she knew it was just a mask and that behind his wrinkled exterior, his mind was as sharp as a tack.

Mr. Morrow watched as Larry Lovell slowly ascended the grand staircase. Fairday followed him as he gingerly took each step, using his cane and hanging on tightly to the banister. She turned and gave her father a wistful smile, which he returned with a farewell wave of the dishrag.

The instant Mr. Morrow was out of sight, the crotchety man struggling to get up the steps suddenly quickened his pace. He lifted his cane and bounded down the hallway, taking long, easy strides all the way to the door at the end. Fairday couldn't believe her eyes! She had to trot just to keep up with him. He really did play the part of the grumpy curmudgeon well.

When they reached the door, he stopped and turned to face her, his blue eyes sparkling. "I must thank you, Miss Morrow."

"Thank me?" Fairday asked. "Thank me for what?"

"Thank you for giving me the opportunity to find out what went on in this house. It's been a mystery I've wanted to solve for many, many years." He placed a hand on her shoulder, and she opened the door.

# THIRTY-SIX

## FRIEND OR FOE?

Fairday rushed into the room with Larry Lovell close on her heels. She had wanted to point out the mirror as they passed by it but knew there were more pressing issues at the moment. Lizzy and Marcus looked up in surprise, and Fairday could tell from their expressions that they were feeling the pressure.

"How is she?" Fairday asked.

"Very unhappy, as far as I can tell," Marcus responded with a grimace. "She's been clawing the armrest to pieces and mumbling to herself."

Lizzy began to explain, "We, uh, left the sheet on her because we had no idea if your dad would be with you, Fairday." She glanced up uncomfortably, adding, "Um, hi,

Mr. Lovell—sure glad it's you. By the way, I'm Lizzy, and this is Marcus." She indicated Marcus with a wave of her arm.

Larry briskly nodded, tipping his hat to both of them as he strode across the room. Fairday's brain was whirring as he approached the concealed figure. Taking a deep breath to calm herself, she hurried to follow him and, with nervous fingers, whipped off the sheet with one great swish, exposing their captive.

Ruby looked wretched. Her face was set in a scowl and her skeletal fingers had scratched out long trails in the armrests of the chair. Shifting her dark eyes upward, she met Larry Lovell's gaze. And just for an instant, an unseen current of static electricity seemed to spark between them. Suddenly, Ruby's wrinkled face pulled back into a sneer as she spat out, "It's you!"

"You know each other?" Lizzy asked.

Larry replied, "To be honest, I'm . . . I'm not sure. You said you had Ruby Begonia, but this"—he hesitated—"*person* looks nothing like the girl I once knew. How did you manage to tie her up like this?" he asked, eyeing the writhing ribbons holding her prisoner.

Fairday began to explain about the blueprints and the spell that Marcus had used but was interrupted by a drawling, raspy voice.

"We certainly *do* know each other," Ruby hissed, straining against the ribbons holding her down. "Just because you don't recognize me in this hideous state does not erase the past!"

Quickly turning to face Fairday, Larry asked her seriously, "How can you be sure your captive is, in fact, Ruby Begonia? Do you have any concrete proof?"

Ruby's lips turned up in a crude leer. "You need proof that I am indeed Ruby Begonia?"

"Yes, I think that's in order. Wouldn't you agree, Miss Morrow?" Larry asked.

Fairday jolted to attention, startled by the sound of her name popping up. "I . . . uh . . . well, yes, I think we should have some proof that you are who you say you are," she said, her voice rising in confidence at Larry's approving nod. Lizzy was mouthing, "Yes, yes, definitely."

"Very well, Larry Lovell." Ruby drew out the syllables as she spoke his name. "Do you remember when we were children and you were accused of stealing a loaf of bread from Bigford's Grocery?" She casually leaned back into the cushions, her black eyes holding his. "Who was it that came to your rescue that day?"

In stunned silence, he stared at her. Fairday felt like she was on pins and needles, the energy in the room pulsating at a heightened frequency as they anxiously awaited his response.

His face softened around the edges, and when he spoke, it was in earnest. "It was you, Ruby Begonia. I have never told anyone about that incident." He paused, then asked in a confused voice, "Why, then, are you acting so hateful toward me?"

"You are the reason I have been trapped up here for all these years! I have been a prisoner, lost between reality and time, destined to be alone for what has felt like an eternity! It was you, Larry Lovell, who padlocked the door at the end of the hall!" she accused him.

A dawning expression washed over his face and he exclaimed, "That was your voice I heard that day?" He shook his head in disbelief. "My God, I never knew."

"This is killing me!" Marcus shouted. "Will someone please let us in on the big secret already? I can't stand the suspense any longer!"

The sudden outburst broke through the thick wall of tension that had built up, and Lizzy let out a deep breath, her face relaxing as she shot Fairday the "thank God someone said something" look.

"Do you remember the article we discussed, Miss Morrow?" he asked.

"'The Missing Bride'?" she answered.

"Originally, that article was intended to cover the magnificent wedding scheduled to take place. But after the bride went missing, the headline unfortunately changed." He cast his gaze downward, adding, "I was there—the day you disappeared. I covered the story." His eyes met Ruby's once again, and he cleared his throat. "Twenty years later, I covered the death of your father, Thurston. A few months after the tragic incident, I was driving past the Begonia House and noticed the gate was ajar. I drove up to the house and found the front door open as well. 'That's odd,' I thought, and decided to have a look."

"Yes, yes! Finally getting there. Remembering everything clear as day now, are we?" Ruby muttered. "Not a very good day for you, though, was it?"

"No, no, it wasn't." His expression turned grim as he added darkly, "I came very close to dying that day."

"And it's more of my bad luck that the tree didn't succeed in dragging you to your death." Ruby glowered at him.

"The willow?" Lizzy asked.

"Yes," Larry replied. "That wicked willow almost took my life." He paused, then added, "But it did take another life, didn't it, Miss Begonia?"

Ruby hung her head at his words and began to weep.

Fairday remembered thinking the willow tree could have killed Thurston Begonia. Had she been correct in that assumption? Thoughts spiraled madly around in her head. Suddenly, a ringing bell went off in a distant corner of her brain. Her internal alarm system was beeping incessantly, reminding her that it wouldn't be long before they had to sit down to a perfectly normal dinner. Would the DMS be able to figure it all out in time?

# THIRTY-SEVEN

## TWO SIDES TO EVERY STORY

The sound of Ruby's choking sobs silenced the bell going off in her head, and Fairday turned her attention back to the present. She knew this situation had to play out at its own pace. All she could do was pray there would be enough time left to come up with some sort of genius plan that would leave them safe and enable her to explain everything to her parents.

Ruby looked up from underneath matted gray hair and whispered through clenched teeth, "I tried to warn him. I tried to save my father, but I was too late. I watched as the branches threw him to the ground below. I heard his bones snap when he hit." The icy words fell from her lips.

A crucial piece of the puzzle had just fit into place. Larry had told Fairday that Thurston's death had gone unsolved all these years. Now only they knew the truth about how he had died, though she highly doubted any of them would ever report it to the authorities. Besides, what court of law was going to send a tree to jail, even if it did prove to be deadly? But why did it murder him? What kind of evil magic was needed to cause a tree to rip apart anyone who looked down on it? That wasn't completely true. It had only attacked when the brass key had been used. She remembered her father opening the door to the balcony, and they had both peered out and nothing had happened. The willow didn't so much as shift in the breeze. So the willow trying to grab them definitely had to do with the brass key. The scribbled note on the back of the picture read: *Beware the tree when you use the key.* Her racing thoughts on the subject were cut short as Marcus spoke up.

"So it was the willow that killed Thurston Begonia?" Marcus asked.

"That appears to be the case, yes," Larry replied.

"And it almost got you too?" Marcus asked again, his eyebrows raised.

"Yes, it almost got me too," Larry answered. There was a moment of tense quiet as he removed his glasses, wiped the lenses clean, and adjusted them back onto his face. Clearing his throat, he said, "So now, where was I? Ah, yes! After Thurston Begonia died, I came back to the house out of curiosity. The police were done investigating and the home had been packed away, except for a few scattered pieces of furniture here and there. I was standing in the empty foyer when I heard strange music coming from somewhere upstairs."

Fairday's heart skipped a beat. He had heard it too! Lizzy shot her a startled look, then nudged Marcus in the side.

"It sounded like someone playing the bagpipes, though the notes were somewhat off," he added thoughtfully. "I followed the music up the spiral stairs and into this room. But there was no one there. Suddenly, I realized I could no longer hear the music and thought perhaps I had been imagining things. So I decided to poke around for a bit."

Larry began to pace back and forth. He scratched his chin thoughtfully, clearly trying to remember all the details of that fateful day. With each contemplative step came a click of his cane connecting dully with the wood floor.

"I poked around for some time, and when I turned to leave, I noticed a key hanging from the lock on the other door. Naturally, I walked over to investigate. I turned the key and stepped out onto the balcony. Leaning over the railing, I tried to get a glimpse of the spot where Thurston's body had fallen, and at that instant, the willow sprang to life. Its twisted branches were glowing blue, growing right before my eyes and rising up to where I stood. Faster and faster, they extended upward, one after the other. Sharp twigs pierced my skin as they began to wrap tightly around my body, scratching and ripping through my clothes." He was motioning furiously with his hands, reenacting what it was like to be trapped inside a tangled web of angry, prob-ing branches.

"That is one scary willow," Marcus said.

"I struggled to pull myself free and finally managed to es-cape from their clutches!" he exclaimed, yanking an invis-ible limb off his chest. "Then I slammed the door and shut them out." The air in the room was very still as all present reflected on their own feelings regarding the murderous willow tree.

"What then, Larry? Tell them what you did next," Ruby said acidly. Her crooked mouth coiled into a horrible gri-mace as she shot daggers at him with her eyes.

He seemed unsettled as he replied, "I . . . why, I ran, of course. I ran out to my car."

"But you didn't drive away, did you? No! You chose to come back and meddle in things you couldn't possibly un-derstand. I watched as you padlocked the door. I watched as you sealed my fate."

"How . . . how was I to know you were trapped some-where in this house?" he stammered, sounding baffled.

"I screamed for you to stop!" she bellowed. "I yelled with all my might. I made the walls amplify my voice a hun-dred times—it shook the floors. It rattled the paintings!" Her chest was heaving as she glared menacingly up at him.

"I remember. I was scared half to death," he responded gravely. "I had no idea that was your voice. I . . . I'm not sure what I thought it was." Larry shook his head. "I was beside myself after the tree tried to kill me. So much so that I mustered up the courage to come back in here and padlock the door to keep out curious trespassers, like myself, who would find themselves in a whole heap of trouble with that willow. Just as I was fastening the lock on the door, I heard a terrible cry. The whole house seemed to shriek at me to STOP! I hurried to secure the lock, then fled, and I have never been back since. . . ." He paused. "Until now." He peered at them from behind his glasses. His story seemed to weave around them like a sticky web. "I knew that I would never tell anyone about what had happened. Who in the world would ever believe such a far-fetched story?"

Fairday understood exactly where he was coming from and suddenly felt incredibly lucky to have Lizzy and Marcus on her side, witnessing everything right along with her. Having third-party confirmation really helps when you're trying to prove to someone that you're not completely mental.

Larry continued. "After a while, I put the whole thing out of my head and gave the padlock key to the police. I told them I had locked the door to the third floor, that the balcony was dangerous and in need of repair."

Fairday clearly remembered the anticipation she had felt when her father had popped open the padlock. And when they saw the dilapidated balcony, Fairday didn't hesitate to promise she would stay off it as her father defined the word *intimidating*: someone or something filling you with fear. He had sure nailed that one.

# THIRTY-EIGHT

## A SORTED PAIR

The sunlight was diminishing, and darkness crept in around them. Elongated shadows shifted across the room as the day was muted by the impending evening. Fairday had been so caught up in the story she hadn't even noticed the fading light. She suddenly realized she had been squinting. Marcus seemed to read her mind and walked over to switch on the lamp. Soft yellow light flooded the room, lifting the hazy fuzziness, and Fairday relaxed her eyes as the scene came back into focus.

Larry picked up a crate and carried it over to Ruby. Once he was settled, he looked into Ruby's eyes and in a consoling voice said, "So you see, Miss Begonia, it was never my intention to trap you—I was trying to lock up the third floor so no one else would suffer the same fate as your father. I certainly had no idea I was sealing your fate. I am truly sorry that you've been stuck up here, alone for . . . oh, what has it been now?" He paused. "I would say it must be about fifty-six years. That is, until Miss Morrow came along."

"Fifty-seven years, actually. Fifty-seven long, painful, mind-numbing years," Ruby answered sourly.

Fairday couldn't even begin to fathom what it would feel like to be trapped alone for all those years. What would she do all day? She always wished for more time to read, but certainly not like that! How terrible it must have been for Ruby! Her heart ached at the notion as she considered the disheveled woman strapped to the chair in front of her.

"What happened to you?" Lizzy asked gently. All eyes and ears locked on Ruby Begonia, anticipating her answer.

The bitter wall that seemed to surround Ruby began to crumble away as she spoke in a faraway voice. "My time is running out as we speak," she said sadly.

"What do you mean?" Marcus asked.

"Every second I spend on this side of the house brings me closer to my death. When the red sand in the hourglass you found runs out, I will die."

"Is that why you never tried to escape?" Lizzy asked.

"I did try, for many years. But each time I had to keep the hourglass in mind. I never got very far."

Still listening, Fairday took the hourglass out of her DMS

pack and placed it on the table. The sand was falling slowly, and there were less than a handful of grains left to drop.

"Does the sand only move when you're on this side of the house?" Fairday asked. Her mind flashed back to when she and Lizzy had witnessed the hourglass start working. She suddenly knew who had been outside the tent. *That's why the sand started falling! Ruby was in my room!* A shiver ran down her spine at the thought. Glancing at Lizzy, she could tell by the look on her face that her friend was coming to the same conclusion.

"Yes, and that's what really kept me a prisoner of this house," Ruby said. Turning to Larry, she sighed deeply. "I'm sorry for blaming you all these years. It wasn't your fault. You just did what any good person would have done."

"I'm still confused. How is your life tied to the grains of sand in the hourglass?" Larry asked.

Ruby opened her mouth to answer, but Fairday interrupted. "Um, excuse me, but don't we need to get you back to the other side, like right now?"

"No, my dear, don't worry. I now know that time spent with others is more valuable than an eternity alone," Ruby said.

Fairday let Ruby's words sink in and couldn't help but wonder if she would be as calm if she knew *her* time was almost up. She wasn't sure, but she knew she definitely wouldn't want to spend forever by herself.

"Is the hourglass the reason you went missing?" Marcus asked.

"No, other events took place on my wedding day that led me to this fate," Ruby answered wearily.

"What *did* happen on the day of your wedding?" Larry asked. "There were so many people in attendance. It seemed unbelievable that you were never found, that not a single soul had any clue as to what might have happened to you."

"My wedding, ha! As if I ever wanted to get married! That would have just been another endless imprisonment— trapped in this town forever," Ruby said.

"You never wanted to get married? What about Gilford Pomfrey?" Lizzy asked.

Fairday shot her an impressed look, amazed that her friend had remembered the groom's name from the news-paper article.

"No, I did not want to marry Gilford," she said. "The meaningless lifestyle that came neatly packaged with his marriage proposal was not what I wanted. My greatest de-sire was to travel the world." She sighed deeply, casting her eyes downward. "Growing up in high society can be very dreary, not to mention very, very lonely."

Ruby snapped her head up and stared blankly into the room. Her dark eyes were distant, and the tone of her voice quickly turned icy as she continued. "It was my father who wanted me to marry Gilford. He demanded it of me. He told me it was for my own safety. I had no way out! I couldn't just run away. Where would I go? What would I do? I felt . . . trapped."

Marcus looked puzzled. "But you were going to marry him, right?" he said. "On that day, if whatever happened hadn't happened, you would have gone through with it?"

"Yes," she said. "I would have married Gilford. For what it's worth, I always wanted to make my father proud." Shaking her head, she went on. "I was prepared to hand myself over, even though my greatest desire was just to be free—free of Gilford, free of my father and this house, free of my mundane life."

Larry muffled a cough and then said, "But you never showed that to anyone. You always seemed happy. I interviewed the wedding photographer for the news article. He told me you had been looking forward to getting married."

"Yes, I was having my photograph taken for my father. I wanted him to have a memory of me, just as I was, before I became Mrs. Gilford Pomfrey."

"We know you had your picture taken in this very room. In fact, you were sitting in the same striped chair," Fairday said.

"That's true, though it was over there." Ruby lifted a long finger and pointed to the corner of the room opposite the door.

Fairday exchanged a look with Lizzy and understood exactly what she was talking about. It was Lizzy who asked the question that had been formulating in Fairday's brain. "What were you pointing to in the picture?"

Keeping her eyes on Lizzy, Ruby began retelling the story

of the day she disappeared. "I saw my diary in your back-pack, so I assume you know about the gypsy. It was Eldrich I was pointing at when the photographer snapped the portrait. I saw her standing in the doorway watching me. He said something, and my gaze shot away from her for a second. When I looked back, she was gone. I had no idea what *that* woman was doing at my wedding. Certainly, my father wouldn't have invited her. I was distracted as the photographer packed up his equipment and bid me farewell."

"So what was she doing there?" Marcus asked.

"After the photographer left, she reappeared from out of nowhere. In her slithering voice, she formally introduced herself and said, 'I've an offer for you, something to think through.' Then, lifting the hem of her dress, she revealed the bejeweled high-heeled sneakers.

"I was captivated by their brilliance. I had seen them as a young girl and didn't think I'd ever see them again. I hardly noticed as she lowered herself onto my bed, smoothing out the coverlet with her long fingers, and beckoned for me to come closer."

Fairday was biting her nails as Ruby described the scene. She could envision the eerie bedroom—the flickering candles on the vanity, the red velvet coverlet.

Suddenly, Ruby bellowed, "Oh, why did I listen to her? Why did I ever agree to her offer?"

"What was it? What did you agree to?" Marcus asked.

"She said she had something for me. Something my

father wanted me to have. 'I would not be offering you this fabled prize if you were not the apple of your father's eye.' Those were her exact words. Well, I had to know what was so important, so I asked why she had come. 'Let me show you,' she said in a mischievous voice. I remember the innocent tilt of her head and the secret way she smiled at me. In an instant she was gliding out of the room and onto the balcony. I followed right behind her, rapt with excitement.

"With a wink of her eye, she leaped over the railing. Before I knew what hit me, I realized she was flying! It was unbelievable! She soared through the clouds, flipping and spinning gracefully before anyone outside noticed. I remember her whizzing by and then landing next to me. 'How?' I asked.

"Eldrich held out a foot and wiggled it. 'The sneakers have the power to fly. They are the reason I can soar through the sky.' Her voice was dripping with venom, but I couldn't hear it! I was blinded by the high-heeled sneakers and what they could do for me. It was my way out. I had to have them. I wanted them to be mine."

Fairday, Lizzy, and Marcus shot each other incredulous looks. "The sneakers can make you fly?" The words came out of Fairday's mouth first.

"Oh yes, they can fly," Ruby said. "And, my dear, they can do much more than just that."

# ~THIRTY-NINE~

## NO MORE, NO LESS

Lizzy was shaking her curls, muttering, "I just don't believe it."

Larry's expression was unreadable as he asked Ruby in a serious voice, "What was her offer?"

"Why, Eldrich offered me the high-heeled sneakers, of course," Ruby said bitterly, twirling the ribbons faster and faster.

"But did the gypsy want anything for them?" Marcus asked.

"Of course she wanted something," Ruby replied. "Eldrich told me I could have the sneakers for what she called a trade of sorts."

"A trade?" Fairday repeated. She couldn't imagine

anything she owned that would be a good enough swap for flying, bejeweled sneakers. *I mean, really, what's cooler than that!*

"Yes, a trade," Ruby said. "Eldrich explained that in exchange for the sneakers, she would acquire my natural gifts. Well, I had no idea what she was talking about, but I knew I wanted the shoes. I was bewitched! I didn't pay any real attention to what was said. 'For the shoes, I bid you farewell. They are yours, use them well. Now to claim what must be mine, your beauty and song I take this time.'"

Fairday thought about the terms of the trade. Would she give up her beauty and song in exchange for sneakers that could make you fly? Well, she wasn't exactly a supermodel and currently had zero musical talent. What would be the harm? The choice seemed so obvious. But on second thought, maybe those terms should be taken more seriously.

"Once they were in my possession, my skin started to crawl, and my insides felt like they had turned to sour milk. I ignored it. I didn't care. I was going to fly! I could almost feel the wind in my hair as I bent down to put the sneakers on. But just as quickly, I realized they didn't fit. I pushed and squeezed, but they were much too small. As you can well see." Ruby nodded down at her swollen feet.

"I was incensed! My prospects of flying began to disappear as it dawned on me that the shoes would never fit! What had I just agreed to? I yelled at her, but she just stood there grinning at me heartlessly. 'You agreed to my terms,'

Eldrich said. 'The shoes you possess—a trade is a trade, no more, no less.' I ran to the mirror to check my reflection. My hair was duller and my skin began to turn ashen. 'The debt that was owed has now been repaid,' she laughed. 'The score has been settled because of your trade. I took what you gave in exchange for those shoes. Consider yourself lucky that I allowed you to choose.' Eldrich was changing as well. Her wrinkled skin was smoother, and her hair was no longer a tangled mat. I pleaded with her, but by that time, she had transformed into a beautiful woman, and I had become this." Ruby's head lolled back as she bellowed, "I became a monster!"

"You're not a monster," Lizzy said with softness in her voice.

"Eldrich reminded me of the key. That I could choose to go through the mirror to the other side. I knew what she was talking about. As you know from my diary, I had hidden the key long ago. My father never knew I'd found it."

"So when Eldrich reminded you about the key, was she suggesting you would stay forever as you were before you made the trade?" Lizzy asked.

"Yes," Ruby said. "But there was a string attached. I would remain young on the other side, with all the time in the world. However, should I choose to come back, my time here would be limited by the sands in the hourglass."

Larry said, "So that's the choice you made—to stay forever as you were but to live only as a reflection."

Nodding, she said, "My mind was settled. I couldn't possibly let anyone see me in this hideous state! I was prepared to go through the mirror, but before I entered, Eldrich heeded a final warning: 'If on the other side is where you dwell, you will remain the self you know so well. But should you choose to leave that place, you will die with this face.' And hearing her words, I knew if I ever came out, this is how I would appear until the sand ran out."

Fairday shivered. *How horrible,* she thought. Flicking her eyes at the hourglass, she watched another red grain fall. Would she have made the same choice and hidden for all those years? "But you could have told your father what had happened. I mean, he wouldn't have thrown you out or anything just because you weren't beautiful anymore, would he?" She knew in her heart that her father would never have cared about what she looked like; he would have just wanted her to be safe.

Lizzy's brain seemed to be percolating as she asked, "But your dad knew how the brass key worked, right? You wrote that he wore it around his neck, until he threw it at Eldrich and lost it."

"Yes!" Ruby exclaimed, bolting upright in her seat. "I knew he understood the magic. The gypsy had created the blueprints for *him.* I planned to reveal myself through the mirror when I was ready. Then I could explain what happened before he had to see me like . . . like this."

"But how come you weren't able to communicate with

him *where* you were? Thurston Begonia wasted away in this house—he never came out, never spoke to anyone," Larry questioned.

"It was all part of the enchantment. Later on, I realized my father couldn't see or hear me. Eldrich also warned me that in twenty years, on the day the magic lifted, I would weep while I watched the willow claim him."

Fairday's mind skipped to the warning written on the back of the photo as she asked, "Was that why you wrote on the back of the picture? Were you trying to tell him something about the tree?"

Ruby looked sad, sighing deeply before she said, "Yes, I tried to warn him. True to Eldrich's words, exactly twenty years after we had been living side by side, in two separate worlds, my father could finally see me."

"What, were you like standing right next to him or something?" Marcus interrupted.

"In a way," Ruby said. "As it just so happened that the day the enchantment lifted, my father was in this room, sitting in this same chair, looking at my picture. He did that often."

"The one in the oval frame?" Lizzy asked.

"Correct. I had sneaked over and taken a copy of that picture so I could use the magic to watch my father, which made me feel closer to him. On that day, I was looking through it." Ruby sighed.

"Your dad knew you were always nearby, right?" Fairday asked, remembering the letter they had found.

"Yes," she said. "That's why when the curse lifted, he instantly realized I was there. Suddenly, I recalled Eldrich's warning. I had no idea what was going to happen, only that it had something to do with the willow tree. In my haste, I tried signaling him through the picture, flashing my eyes toward the mirror." Her voice rose steadily as she went on. "I knew I couldn't use the wardrobe. He would never have recognized me—I would have scared him half to death if I popped out looking like this. Besides, I knew he *understood* how to use the brass key. My father found it after I went missing, and always had it with him. I yelled out that he was in danger, and the house's magic imprinted my words on the back of the picture. When I saw what was happening, I hoped he'd turn it over *before* he used the key to open the door."

"I guess he didn't notice the 'beware the tree' part," Fairday said quietly.

"No. As soon as he saw my image move, he bolted out of the chair. I flew out of my room just as he opened the balcony door and turned to face the mirror." Tears glistened in the corners of her eyes as she whispered, "And then he saw me."

A heavy gloom seemed to descend over them as Ruby continued. "His eyes lit up as they looked into mine. But before I could say anything, a bluish glow began to fill the room. The branches from the willow were coming in through the balcony. I watched him as he fought for his life. I had to call for help, so I went through the mirror. He didn't notice as I swept past and raced down the stairs." Tears began to flow freely down her gaunt face.

"The anonymous phone call to the police!" Larry blurted out. "Detectives were baffled by it for ages. No one could ever figure out who had called!"

"Yes, it was me," Ruby replied. "After I notified the police, I hurried back up the spiral staircase to help him. But when he saw me, he froze. I had forgotten what I looked like and called out to him. In his moment of shock, a branch grabbed hold of him." The torment in her voice seemed endless as she whispered, "My picture was still clenched in his hand as he fell. I heard his scream cut short, and I knew he was dead."

"Wow," Marcus whispered. "Someone needs to cut down that tree."

# FORTY

## THE FINAL PIECE OF THE PUZZLE

"So you still don't know why Eldrich wanted revenge?" Lizzy asked. "I mean, was it because he didn't pay her for the blueprints? What was their price?"

"I asked myself that same question for many years. Why? Why had this happened to me? What had I ever done to deserve this? I never discovered the answer, though I have never stopped wondering how my father came to know Eldrich and have the blueprints created. My father couldn't see me, but I could watch him. I saw him try to rekindle the house's magic, but it didn't seem to work."

"Speaking of magic," Marcus said, "how can you make your hair slither like a snake or put us into a trance? I know the house can do all sorts of stuff, but can you too?"

"I'm a part of the Begonia House," she replied. "Its magic is my magic—but only on the other side of the mirror."

"We might be able to give you a little information about how your father met Eldrich and why the family was cursed. He explains it in this letter to you, but I'm guessing you never saw it." Fairday dug in her bag for the letter and handed it to Ruby.

Ruby carefully unfolded it and began reading. Fairday wanted to give her some privacy, but she couldn't pull her eyes away from the scene. Finally, Ruby lifted her head, tears glistening in her eyes again. "Thank you. This does help answer some of the questions I've spent my life thinking about. Where did you find this?" Ruby asked.

"I found it in a box of bills," Marcus replied.

"I guess I was preoccupied when I came to this side, always trying to use only a little of the precious time I had left in the real world. Time, as you know, is stopped on the other side of the mirror," Ruby said.

"It's always three o'clock on your wedding day," Lizzy clarified.

"That's correct," Ruby responded.

Fairday's eyes shifted to the hourglass, just as another grain fell. There weren't many left.

Lizzy broke through the stillness that had enveloped them. "So are you stuck like this forever now? Isn't there some way to undo the trade?" she asked.

Ruby eyed her curiously. "Eldrich did give me one final

piece of the puzzle. She told me if I were to ever give the shoes away to someone who fit into them, I would be free."

"Free?" Lizzy repeated.

"Yes, free. I would become myself again," Ruby explained.

"Yourself, like you were when you were younger?" Fairday asked.

"I have absolutely no idea what would happen. Obviously, I have yet to find anyone who could wear them," Ruby answered.

"Is *that* why you've been haunting us?" Lizzy asked.

"Yes, I wanted to trap you," she said. "But you three managed to escape. I did my best to entice you to the other side in hopes of breaking the curse. I thought you'd try to get your book back, and when you didn't come, I took your dog. Don't worry, I tucked your book safely on a shelf in my father's study."

"Thanks. It's my favorite story," Fairday said, breathing a sigh of relief that she'd get her prized possession back soon. "So all this time you've been looking for someone to try the shoes on?"

"Yes, but my time is almost up."

"Well, you're not going to believe this, but . . . uh . . . actually, the sneakers fit me." Lizzy's words bounced through the room like overly heated particles.

"They do?" Ruby looked strangely optimistic.

"They sure do," Fairday said. "Just like Dorothy's ruby slippers."

An anxious excitement filled the room. Once the chair released Ruby, she handed over the high-heeled sneakers. No one could guess what was going to happen, but Lizzy accepted the gift, sliding them on right before the last grains of sand fell through the hourglass.

Fairday watched the trees blur by in shades of red, yellow, and gold as the bus rumbled toward school. It was Monday, and everything was perfectly normal in the quiet country town of Ashpot. As she settled into her seat, she could hear the usual laughter and whispering that went along with the morning bus ride.

Smiling to herself, she recalled the weekend's events as the bus trundled down the road. Lizzy's face had been priceless as she swooped and swirled around the third-floor room, wearing the high-heeled sneakers. Even Ruby had watched in amazement as she whipped by, laughing gleefully.

After Ruby had given the sneakers to Lizzy, the enchantment broke. The red sand in the hourglass turned green and Ruby transformed back into herself, though she was much older now. Her black eyes became a more natural green, and her hair was silver and white, though streaked with hints of red.

The bus went over a whopping pothole and Fairday burst

out laughing as she bounced out of her seat and landed back down with a thump. Her father had gone on and on about the charming, older lady who had mysteriously joined them for dinner Saturday night. It was quite a tale the DMS had to come up with in order to explain her presence. But after all was said and done, he had bought it. Larry promised he would look after Ruby, and when she left the Begonia House with him that night, she looked more cheerful than she had in a very, very long time.

Fairday recalled something her father had said while they were moving in. He had predicted that moving into the Begonia House was going to be a real adventure. If this last case was any indication, she knew the DMS was going to be busy over the next year. After all, she lived in a magical house, which came with really cool instructions; Lizzy had amazing high-heeled sneakers that could make her fly; and they had initiated an awesome new member into their club, whose father just happened to be an FBI agent. Not to mention they had met two useful contacts to help them solve future cases: Larry Lovell, investigative journalist, and Ruby Begonia, the no-longer-missing bride. Plus, they had each learned something about themselves, just like the characters in her favorite book. Things were pretty darn good!

The bus pulled up to the front of the school and Fairday grabbed her backpack. As she hopped off the last step, she caught Marcus's eye in the crowd. He immediately began pushing his way through the throng of kids and slipped in next to her.

"So the DMS is meeting again this Saturday?" he whispered.

"Yeah," Fairday replied. "Be at my front gates at noon." She glanced around to check that no one was watching, then leaned into Marcus. "Lizzy said she's figured it all out, and she's going to use the sneakers to fly over. Get ready, because you're not going to believe what I found."

"Fear not the unexpected, right?" Marcus smirked.

"Exactly!" Fairday exclaimed as they merged into the crowd of kids and disappeared inside the brick building.

# ACKNOWLEDGMENTS

This has been an incredible adventure so far, and we couldn't have done it without a whole cast of characters.

We'd like to begin with our amazing editor, Krista Vitola. Her attention to detail is brilliant, and because of her comments and suggestions we were able to bring Fairday's story to greater heights. Krista's willingness to work with us, even though we were new authors, is truly appreciated. We'd like to thank Roman Muradov. His illustrations are unique and capture the mystery perfectly. We'd also like to mention our copy editors for their keen eyes and the way they polished the story to a shine. We are so lucky to get to work with the wonderful people at Delacorte Press.

We can't imagine a better agent than Rachael Dugas, from Talcott Notch Literary. Her determination and enthusiasm were just what we needed. Hearing her thoughts on our characters made our hearts soar. Thank goodness we connected with Gina Panettieri at a writing conference and she passed our manuscript on to Rachael.

Thank you to our family and friends. Between us there are too many to list, but we know you know who you are! Your love, encouragement, and support have meant so much to us. Knowing you were behind us helped us to pursue our dreams.

We read the first version of our book to Mrs. Robinson's class many years ago, and each year we have read it to a new group of students. Their feedback has helped our story grow and change. There's nothing more exciting than hearing from young readers. We were lucky enough to have our very own test audience, and we are so grateful for their honesty.

The bloggers and authors we met online and in person have given us feedback that has made us better writers. Their words allowed us to see our writing through a different lens, and although it was tough at first, we were able to take their advice and rise to the challenge. The writing community is filled with strong, inspirational people, and it has been magical sharing stories with friends across the world.

To those of you who agreed to read and edit the story in any of its various stages: you are the best, and we know we had a lot to learn!

Connecticut schools Flanders Elementary in Southington, Hop Brook Elementary in Naugatuck, and Middlebury Elementary in Middlebury each welcomed us and allowed us to share our book with their students. What a thrill it was talking to kids, teachers, parents, and librarians about our writing process.

Living with a writer can't be easy. While the crazy ideas are brewing, time is dedicated to writing, editing, and collaborating. This means other chores and obligations might be put aside. A special thank-you to Ron and James, not only for being patient with us through the winding journey that led us to this point, but for their constant love and support.

Lastly, we'd both like to thank the best coauthor anyone could ever ask for. Fear not the unexpected, right?

# YEARLING

*Turning children into readers for more than fifty years.*

## Classic and award-winning literature for every shelf.
## How many have you checked out?

**Find the perfect book, play games,
and meet favorite authors at RandomHouseKids.com!**